FOUND BY the WATER

Shirley A Genovese   Cynthia Gibbs

Watch over each other to make sure that no one misses the revelation of God's grace. And make sure no one lives with a root of bitterness sprouting within them which will only cause trouble and poison the hearts of many. Hebrews 12:15-16 TPT

DEDICATION

To Our Husbands & Hearts
CHARLES A. GENOVESE
NORMAN P. GIBBS, SR

To Our Sister-Forever Loved
LYNNETTE S. OWENS

Contents

PREFACE

*F*ound By the Water is an allegory written as contemporary fiction, inspired by a lone woman's unexpected encounter at Jacob's Well in ancient Samaria.[1] The story begins in the late spring of the early twenty-first century in Rocky Mountain territory now known as northern Idaho. Settlers migrated from the east two centuries ago. Constant conflict over water has strained the harmony between the communities.

You will meet Anna Marin and Brea Duncan, with Robert Marineta, and his son Joshua; as well as others who live and work in neighboring towns. Anna is the young matriarch of the valley town of Marin, who struggles to believe God loves her. Rob and Josh, as they are known, live in the mountain city of Bellalto. From the beginning, Rob's family has been in control of the area's most abundant natural resource, water. Josh has recently joined the family's privately owned Chute Valley Water Authority. Both men have a desire to break the cycle of greed and bitterness which has developed and caused division for over a hundred and fifty years. Anna and Josh meet under challenging circumstances.

How will God reveal his love for Anna and will she embrace it? Will Rob and Josh succeed in their efforts? Is it possible to break the power of generational bitterness?

Sometimes God has purposes that we will only understand when we see him face to face. We created Found By the Water to both entertain and encourage you by the life changing power of God's love and words, woven into an engaging story.

Note: Scripture references are provided in the Appendix.

CHARACTERS

~ROBERT (Rob) MARINETA: Patriarch of the Marineta family who were the founders of Bellalto, a mountain resort town in northern Idaho. Lives in Bellalto. A 59-year-old widower with two grown children. A son, Joshua and a daughter, Madison.
Also:
CEO of the privately held Chute Valley Water Authority (CVWA)
CVWA Board Chair

~ANNA MARIN: Matriarch of the Marin family who were founders of Marin Township located in Chute Valley below Bellalto. Lives in Marin Township. A 43-year-old widow with no children.
Also:
Mayor and Council Chair of Marin Township

~JOSHUA (Josh) MARINETA: Robert Marineta's son, unmarried at 33 years old. Lives in Bellalto.
Also:
Regulatory Compliance Attorney at Law
CVWA Deputy Legal Counsel and Board Member

~BREA DUNCAN: Single at 29 years old. Lives in Marin Township. Army Veteran.
Also:
Member, Marin Town Council
Trip Leader- Pettrie's Bellalto Rafting, a whitewater outfitter. She focuses on leading veterans and others with stress related disorders.
Opinion Editor, *How's Marin Faring* small town newspaper

~ERIC MILLER: Single at 33 years old. Lives in Bellalto.
Also:
Bellalto Building Inspector
Chief, Bellalto Fire Department

~GLEN STUART: Married. 48 years old. He has raised two children with his 43-year-old wife, Meg Stuart. They live in Marin Township. Glen is the former proprietor of Stuart Plumbing.

He is also:

Vice Chair, Marin Town Council

Marin Building Inspector

Chief, Marin Fire Department

~TOM PETTRIE: Scion of the Pettrie business empire in northern Idaho. CVWA's Director of Accounting and Finance. Married. 62 years old. Lives in Bellalto.

~SEAN PETTRIE: Tom Pettrie's son and heir. Employed by his father, Tom, in multiple capacities. Single at 29 years old. Lives in Bellalto.

~DANI EVANS: Sole proprietor of Evans Construction. Single at 32 years old. Lives in Marin Township.

~MARIN TOWN COUNCIL MEMBERS

Mayor and Chair: Anna Marin

Vice Chair: Glen Stuart

Members Mentioned in Meetings

Jacob Denver, Brea Duncan, Sally Redmond, Unnamed Others

~CHUTE VALLEY WATER AUTHORITY (CVWA) BOARD

Chairman: Robert Marineta

Vice Chair: Joshua Marineta

Members Mentioned in Meetings

Tom Pettrie, Mark Thompson, Irene Givens, Unnamed Others

PROLOGUE

Turning to the experienced team of rafters disembarking at the Wild River Café Brea Duncan said, "You aced it today." The café was one of the take-out or terminus points for Bellalto Rafting, a well-known whitewater rafting outfitter. Her admiration for this returning group of battle-worn veterans had grown. As their trip leader that day, she had witnessed navigational teamwork at its finest. It was the only thing she missed about combat; the teamwork needed to survive. Few people knew that she had originally signed on for whitewater rafting after her discharge from the army. She soon learned that the exhilaration and challenges were exactly what she needed to aid the transition, and mild post-traumatic stress disorder (PTSD) reactions, to everyday life. She had been leading trips for six years.

"Hey, Brea. See you next time." They waved and turned toward the café.

Because the adrenaline was still flowing, and would take a while to wear off, Brea decided to drive to headquarters to check on the next trip assigned to her. Feeling hungry after rafting, she picked up her pre-order and walked to her truck. The rafting had kept her fit. At the age of twenty-nine she was small and compact. Her blond curly hair was short for convenience. If she had smiled more, she would have been pretty. The isolation she preferred had become more of a habit than necessity.

'I wonder if I'll catch Sean at HQ tonight.' She thought as she drove and ate. Sean Pettrie was the son and heir apparent of Tom, scion of the Pettrie empire. Whitewater rafting was one of their many business concerns in the region. Brea's personal interests lay in Sean's direction, although he had yet to show he noticed her.

It was after sundown by the time she arrived. There were a handful of cars in the parking lot. The building was dark, except for one or two lighted windows. A few people were still working. Throwing the remains of her meal into the waste basket in the reception area, she walked down the darkened hallway. Brea could hear muffled voices coming through the closed door of Tom's office as she reached the wall-mounted digital display screen of upcoming rafting trips. The voices began to get louder. Slowly she moved closer, noiseless in her rubber soled shoes. Keeping a safe distance away and to the darker areas, she stopped when she could hear clearly. The door was slightly ajar, casting a sliver of light into the corridor.

"I told you something had to be done about Rob Marineta's plans." It was Tom Pettrie. "The water rights belong in Bellalto where they've always been."

"I know, Tom. But I'm not willing to go as far as you are to stop them." The voice was unknown to Brea. It was more of a deep growl full of menace. Footsteps sounded just behind the door and more muffled conversation followed. The door opened and a large man strode past her hiding place toward the exit. She let out the breath she was holding. Tom Pettrie came barreling out following the other man. She shifted deeper into the corner pulling the neck of her shirt over her bright hair just as he headed back to his office. Brea took the opportunity to run out the front door, jump into her truck and flee.

'Whatever that conversation was about, it may be an opening for me. I want time to think.' She thought.

Chapter 1

For such a time as this. Esther 4:14

A small group of mourners stood in a somber circle around Robert and Joshua Marineta by the grave of Michael, their father and grandfather, respectively. As the late afternoon sun sank behind distant peaks, it painted the sky a perfect medley of golds and lavenders. No one standing in the high Rocky Mountain meadow seemed to notice. Only a few tears had fallen as the minister read the eulogy and final prayer. The wild Bella Chute River provided the music. Afterward, people talked in low tones as they slowly followed Rob and Josh, as they were known, on the long path that led to the family home below.

"Big changes are coming, I suppose. Mike was a difficult man."

"He did what he had to do. No sense giving our water away to others."

Gathered in groups in the large dining room, they spoke quietly and looked with expectation at the new family patriarch. Rob was a tall quiet, 59-year-old man, with an air of authority. People loved him for his care of others; traits he had instilled in his son and daughter. Even those who disagreed with him on community issues admired and respected him. He and his late father had not seen eye-to-eye on how to run the family business, the privately owned Chute Valley Water Authority(CVWA). Those living in and around Bellalto and the river valley had opposing views.

Moving confidently among his guests, Rob had a good word for everyone. They stood a little taller when he stepped away and knew he meant every offer of assistance. He would keep his word.

"What are your plans for the water authority, Rob?" Tom Pettrie, a wiry 62-year-old man, interrupted. Rob towered above him. "Are you going to abandon more than a century of good water management?"

Found By the Water

"Josh and I will be talking to the Board at our next meeting, Tom."
Josh, a tall, slender brown-haired man of 33 years, walked over to join the
conversation. There was a strong resemblance to his father including his
commanding blue eyes. Rob put his arm around his son's shoulders. "It's
no secret that we will be making some improvements to how the water is
shared with the valley. We'll talk about this in-depth later. I hope we can
agree on the issues, Tom. Now's not the time. I still haven't spoken to
everyone who came today to honor my father's life." With a quick
handshake, Rob moved away with a smile.

Josh watched his father with admiration. He had been preparing for
years to join him at the Water Authority. For generations, all Marineta
children knew at a young age they had an important responsibility to
uphold. Josh was Rob's first-born. His younger sister, Madison, was still
in law school back east.

Josh had recently returned home after specializing in Regulatory
Compliance at a Boston firm following his graduation from Yale Law.
Now he was back in Bellalto to join the Water Authority as Deputy Legal
Counsel. He was committed to uniting the Chute Valley and Bellalto,
even though he knew the project would be challenging. His plan to start
with the valley town of Marin increased the complexity of the effort.

Sometime later, as the door closed on the last of the guests, Rob turned
to Josh with a smile. "What's on your mind? You've seemed preoccupied
all day."

"I can't help thinking about our efforts to improve regional customer
relations starting in Marin. I'm anticipating a lot of push back from some
of the leaders and our own Board."

"Some will resist more than others. It's understandable. They're good
people brought up on all the old resentments we want to resolve. It'll take
time for them to come around. Thank God we found that old journal."

"I know, Dad. I agree."

"It won't be easy, Josh. But nothing worthwhile ever is. I wish your
mother had lived to join us. She believed in this course of action, too.
Let's rest up for a few days. I'm trusting God is going to work his plan
through us."

They walked together to the kitchen where the caterers were just
finishing the clean-up. Helping themselves to a last cup of coffee and a
sandwich, they sat down at the kitchen table. "Dad let's pray before we

Found By the Water

call it a night." Josh said. "I can stand up in court in defense of a client without a problem. I've learned to keep a professional distance. This new step we're taking is much more personal. It's going to be divisive."

"I know exactly what you mean. It's exciting and unsettling at the same time. We need wisdom to do this the right way."

They bowed their heads and asked God for the help they required to bring an end to the years of hardship in the valley and unify the region.

An hour later, Josh was still awake. He turned on his bedside light and walked to the open window. The night air was fresh and sweet. In the distance, he could hear the rush of the river as it tumbled down the mountains toward the valley below. He reached for the journal Rob had found in a dark corner of the attic, written long ago by a daughter of the first Marineta family, the founders of Bellalto. He opened it randomly and read the fine feathery script written in fading ink.

June 16, 1853 Uncle John and his family have moved to the valley to start a new life without us. I have tried talking to Father about their disagreement. Neither will let go of their anger because each thinks their views are the only way. I long for the days when we first arrived and knew we were home. We all shouted "Bella" (beautiful) at the same time. We fell on our knees and gave thanks to God for bringing us safely to this place where we have thrived. There are plenty of resources for everyone, although Father has changed since we came here from New England. We named our settlement Bellalto because it is a beautiful high place. More people have arrived and we are now a small mountain village with more settlements forming in the valley. We have all been sharing the water. Father is the self-appointed founder and leader in our growing community. He has decided that conservation means that he and Bellalto will control the availability of water. He intends to keep the lion's share for the people in the mountains. I fear this decision will bring hardship to the valley. Uncle believes the Creator gave the water to everyone. Several other families also relocated to lower ground dividing our peaceful society. Lord, what can I do? Please bring us peace and reconciliation. If I did not believe that you know the end from the beginning, I would lose hope.

Josh closed the journal and turned off the light. In the darkness, his prayer echoed that of Elianna Marineta, the journal's author. Peace came as he climbed into bed. He was asleep a moment later.

Chapter 2

Come to me and I will give you rest. Matthew 11:28

In the town of Marin, the slump of Anna Marin's shoulders told the story. Dejection, worry, and discouragement had sculpted her features with more fine lines than most 43-year-old women. She advanced the hose around her garden with water trickling out of it like a slow leak. Weariness showed on her face. *'There's barely enough water to last the month. Good thing the rationing quota starts again soon.'* Anna thought.

The ringing of her cell phone interrupted her thoughts. "Hello, this is Anna." she said. "Matt?" There was a pause to listen and a quick intake of breath. She exhaled attempting to stay calm. To herself she quickly thought, *'It's the same old story. He doesn't come home. He's found someone else to further his own interests.'*

She made a quick decision, that had been a long time coming. "Matt, I'm changing the locks today. Come by tomorrow and pick up your things. They'll be on the porch." She felt surprisingly free. "No! No more talking. It's over." Anna disconnected abruptly.

She walked to the spigot and shut off the water, taking her time to wrap the hose around the reel. The water absorbed quickly into the soil and she knelt to weed the garden rows. Two hours later Anna put her tools away and drained the rest of her water bottle. Wearily, sinking into a chair under a large shade tree, she wiped her forehead with her sleeve and pushed her rich brown hair off her face. A quick glance at the sky showed no sign of rain. It had been dryer than normal. With her head resting on the back of the chair and eyes closed, her thoughts went to better times when she was young and hopeful. *'Ben was taken from me too early. The years we were married were the best of my life.'* A few years her senior, Ben arrived in Marin after buying a nearby farm. They met when he came into the utilities office where she worked after college.

Found By the Water

He asked her to lunch that day and they were married by summer's end. It was the beginning of the good years, until the tractor accident took his life. Focusing on her failures like she often did, she thought. *'I'm a walking disaster when it comes to men. One bad decision after another since Ben died.'*

Ambition had ruled her parents who worked long hours in a misguided loyalty to family heritage. Often left on her own, Anna made sure dinner was on the table and the house was clean. The one joy in her life was her gardens which became her escape from loneliness. They flourished which was not easy in a town without enough water. In addition, as a member of the town's founding family, her parents expected Anna to prepare for her role in town affairs. The day after her sixteenth birthday Anna began a series of jobs during school breaks. Although she had an aptitude for management, she found it hard going. Emulating her parents, she lacked the patience to involve others in problem solving. Her social skills were seriously underdeveloped. To make it worse, Anna seemed unaware of how other people perceived her.

Her real passion was the science and management of growing plants. Her parents had made one unexpected concession during her youth when they allowed her to obtain dual bachelor's degrees in horticulture science and business management from the University of Idaho. Then she came home to carry on the Marin family tradition in town affairs.

She said aloud, "God, are you there? Do you see me?" Startled at the turn of her thoughts, Anna shook her head as if to clear it. "That sounded almost like a prayer!"

Chapter 3

What He sees the Father do He does in like manner. John 5:19

A week later the two Marineta men finished breakfast by a large bay window where the sun created a sparkling rainbow as it shone through the morning mist rising from hanging valleys. "I could watch this view all day, couldn't you?" Rob turned away reluctantly and said to Josh, "Let's firm up our plans this morning. I want to finalize things before the Board meeting this week."

They walked toward Rob's study taking their coffee with them. Settling into comfortably worn leather chairs they gazed out at another eye-catching view. They heard the powerful waterfall through the open window. Their life was all about water conservation and usage rights. Over a century and a half had passed since the Marineta's pioneering ancestors arrived in this region of the Rockies. Since the beginning, the river had been the driving force of the area's economy.

After working for a while Rob yawned, then stood to stretch. He reached for their cups. "I need more coffee."

"Let me." Josh said, "Then I'll tell you my plan for engaging our valley customers."

Rob nodded and sat down with a smile.

Josh soon returned. He set Rob's cup on the table between them. Taking a sip Rob asked, "Thanks. What have you worked out?"

"My strategy is to eventually meet with all the valley town councils. Since we've determined the town of Marin is economically struggling the most, I've decided to start there. Yesterday, I left a message for the Mayor. You know Anna Marin is also the Council Chair. If she is willing to arrange a meeting with the rest of the council it will allow for us to speak face-to face.

Found By the Water

"They'll be able to voice grievances, discuss mutual concerns, and to address their hardship and rancor toward us. Hopefully, there'll be some who are ready for a change."

Rob smiled his agreement. "I like it," he said. "Will you be bringing anyone in to work with you?"

"I'll be asking Eric Miller. My concern is that Anna may not be willing to meet. There's something else I need to mention to you."

"What's that?" Rob asked.

"During my research, I noticed that something was off in the company reports. I couldn't put my finger on it exactly without asking too many questions. I don't want to put anyone on the alert, except you. I think you should discreetly look into it if you have someone you can trust."

"You've confirmed my suspicions and I've already taken some steps to uncover whatever it is. I don't want to involve you now so you can focus on your part of our strategy. But I'll let you know soon what I find."

When Josh got up to leave after they had finished their discussion, he turned back as he reached the door. "Thanks, Dad. I know I can talk to you anytime. It always helps."

Before going to see his friend, Josh decided to take a long walk to clear his mind. He still had a few details to work out. He needed insight and clarity with time alone to pray on how to break through the valley communities deeply ingrained beliefs and emotions about his family.

Entering the woods behind his home he could hear the ever-present sound of the Bella Chute river. By the time it reached the far side of the valley near Marin it was calmer but the current was still strong and fast. Streams ran off in places to form a pristine mountain lake they called Lake Chute.

"Lord, we need hearts that are open to change." Josh prayed aloud as he often did when alone. "Work in all of us for your good purpose. Give me patience. I'll need it." He walked along deep in thought. There was so much he wanted the valley community to know about his father. Especially, how much he cared to give them a better life. Now he had the opportunity.

Taking a path alongside the river, Josh passed the remains of an old, crumbled grist mill. He mentally reviewed all that he had learned through his own research of the region's history. His third great-grandfather, Damian, had come west with his brother John, and their families. Josh had

10

Found By the Water

grown up on the family stories about how they had been heading for the Pacific Ocean. It had been a hard journey and the area was so beautiful they decided to stay. For them, it was a perfect place to call home.

Happy for many years, their families grew and prospered in the mountains. They began to harness the river's power, starting with the gristmill. Eventually, they channeled the water to homes for personal use. In the early years, they routed the water to small individual above-ground reservoirs that served much like wells. Control of water usage became an issue between the brothers. They disagreed about how the river could supply the valley and mountain homes alike. It was a sad story of a fractured family.

After John settled in the fertile valley, with his and other like-minded families, prosperous farms began to fill the landscape. Towns began to form as the valley population increased. John called his town Marin, which attracted agricultural industry because of the river and rich soil. Damian created the Chute Valley Water Authority and built the first dam which enabled Bellalto to develop into a renowned vacation destination and caused the valley prosperity to diminish.

Damian, Joshua's ancestor, had changed after coming to the mountains. He saw his brother as a foolish man who would willingly eschew a potential fortune by sharing the water control. Longing for the tender, loving man of her childhood, his daughter Elianna recorded many stories in her journal of how lies and ill will festered on both sides of the family. She spent her life trying to reconcile them. As she neared the end of her life, she knew her dream would not happen in her lifetime. Her journal grew dusty and forgotten until recently. Rob found it searching the attic for some old files after his father grew ill.

Josh thought back to the prayers Damian's daughter had written. He echoed her sentiments as he spoke into the mountain quietness. "Lord, thank you for raising up a generation in Mom and Dad with the same spirit as Damian's daughter. We want to start a new chapter of being compassionate, kind and forgiving of each other. Show us how to move ahead in making your love known to all the people who live in this region. Let us soon be at peace with everyone. There's so much hurt and anger to address before we can reconcile. Dad and I are committed to this plan. We already face a lot of opposition to any changes and need your strength to move ahead."

Found By the Water

When Josh reached the crest at the great waterfall, he marveled once again at the abundance of God's provision. There was enough for all. He turned to go back home more settled than when he began. Realizing there wasn't enough time to visit Eric due to other commitments, he called him.

"Hi Eric. This is Josh. How are you?" Josh asked, listening to Eric's reply. "Good, glad to hear. Hey, I'd like to run something by you. Are you free for lunch tomorrow? I could meet you at the station at noon. Ok. See you then."

Chapter 4

Everyone has turned to their own way. Isaiah 53:6

Brea Duncan had spent the last few days thinking about her chance encounter at Bellalto Rafting headquarters and the information she had learned while eavesdropping at Tom's office door. The Marinetas were about to do something. Tom's subversion tactic was unsavory enough to deter one rough sounding man from having anything to do with it. Brea's inquisitive mind would not leave the mystery unsolved. She wanted to know what the Marinetas were up to. They only cared for one thing, the Water Authority. Puzzled as to why the scion still worked for the Authority as head of finance and a board member, she decided to ask Sean at the next opportunity.

For now, she wanted to be more important to Sean. He was ambitious and already financially secure, which she wanted in her future. She had learned that they were the same age and shared a common approach to life. Working hard to attract his attention had paid off and now they were spending time together. Today, she had taken care with her personal appearance after finishing her last trip. She cleared the desk she used to arrange the rafting trips with veterans and others with stress disorders. It brought her extra income and kept her near Sean. She knew by first-hand experience the therapeutic qualities of rafting.

"Hey Brea, are you ready?" Sean asked. "Dad told me not to be late."

"Ready." Brea stood. Tonight, she was attending her first party at the Pettrie home. They walked out together passing other women who watched them with envy which, Brea knew from overheard conversations, were motivated more by his family's wealth and connections than anything else.

Found By the Water

Opening the door of his sleek red sports car parked in the executive lot, he helped her in and slid in the driver's side. Giving her an appreciative look, he said. "You look very nice, Brea." She preened at his approval.

They talked about business during the drive to Tom's house. Brea wished she had learned how to flirt. Hoping their relationship could change, she asked him more personal questions than normal. He deflected them easily by responding with questions about her position on the Town Council in Marin, where she lived.

"Have you heard anything about changes in the Water Authority policies?"

"No. What have you heard?"

"Only that there are changes coming and Dad's not happy about it."

It tied with the conversation she had overheard and her heart sank. She was sought out for what she knew, not who she was. She was quiet the rest of the way and stepped out of the car before Sean had a chance to come around to open her door.

Once inside Sean acted the good host and brought her a drink. They drifted to the patio, mingling with other people as the sun set and the sky turned dark. Brea began to relax as she thought about living in a house like Tom's. She imagined herself as Sean's wife and the lifestyle that would come with it.

"Are you here alone?" A well-dressed older woman asked Brea kindly. "Would you like to join us at our table?"

"No, I'm Sean Pettrie's guest. Thank you for the invitation though." Embarrassed, she quickly moved away trying not to look like she was searching for him. She stepped into the house to refresh her drink and wandered around downstairs after checking her appearance in the powder room. Wanting nothing more than to go home, Brea found a comfortable spot to wait for Sean near the central entertaining area. Once more, she heard a conversation in progress from someplace behind her.

"-wants to give the water away. I don't intend to let that happen! Who here is willing to do what it takes to derail him?" She heard Tom Pettrie's raised voice. "What I need is information. I need someone to stall the efforts until we make sure this issue dies and never arises again. Who's with me?"

"What are you doing here?" It was the menacing voice of the man she had previously overheard with Tom. She froze for a second. Then took a

Found By the Water

deep breath before turning around to reply and see who he was. "Don't turn around. It's best you get up and keep walking."

At that moment, Sean opened a door to her left with a frown. Shutting the door behind him, he took in the situation. He gave the man behind Brea a hard look and moved next to her.

"Brea! I'm sorry I was gone so long. I had some business to attend to and you seemed engrossed in a conversation. I'd hoped to be back before you noticed." He said with an ingratiating smile.

"I would like to go home." she replied curtly.

Sean stood watching her for a moment, calculating how much she had overheard. "Ok, let me tell Dad I'll be gone for a bit and we'll leave." As he stepped back into the room, Brea moved away to wait by the front door.

"Who was that?"

"A man who works with my father." Sean replied evasively.

"Is he hired to intimidate guests abandoned by their hosts?" She shot back caustically.

"What were you doing there Brea? That area is private family space."

"I hardly think that private quarters open on to the reception area."

Brea was silent on the remaining ride back to the office, where she had left her truck. Sean took her cue and followed suit. In the parking lot, she opened her door, turned, and said politely. "Thank you for the evening Sean. It wasn't exactly what I hoped it would be but it was gracious of your family to invite me. I enjoyed meeting some interesting people."

Once behind the wheel of her own vehicle, she pulled out without looking back. Rattled by her second encounter with the man who she now realized was a security agent, she thought, *'How could I have pursued it any further without revealing what I overheard the first time I nearly ran into him?'*

"On the other hand, maybe Sean would see me in a different light if I could help stall the Marineta's progress." She spoke aloud. "I am in a perfect position to do that."

Chapter 5

Happy is the man who finds wisdom. Proverbs 3:13

Josh pushed open the door to the Bellalto Fire Department. He walked back to the Chief's office which was empty. "Hey buddy, where are you?" he called.

"Upstairs. Join me." Eric appeared at the top of the stairs. He was the same age and as tall as Josh with the dark hair of his Shoshone-Paiute mother. He was burly and kept fit. Dressed in dusty clothes with cobwebs clinging to his hair, he explained, "I've been deep in history."

"You and me both. What have you found?"

Eric held up a dirty manual. "Remember I told you I wanted to update the fire department's policies and manuals? I'm working on them. I was rummaging around in the archives and I found the original documents from when Bellalto chartered the department. I have an idea that may help you in your quest for reconciliation with the valley."

"Can we talk about it over burgers at Joe's?" Josh knew once Eric's mind was on something, it was hard to get his attention.

"Sounds good. Let me clean up a little. I'll be down in a few minutes."

Eric and Josh were close childhood friends. For a while, Eric had lived with his family. He knew that whatever Eric was going to say would be worth listening to. When Josh went to law school, Eric stayed home. He cared about the area as much as Josh and wanted to make a difference. Recently Eric had become the Fire Chief after proving himself for several years. Still unmarried, as Josh was, he had plenty of time to focus on his passion. That of making Bellalto and the valley a better place to live. They crossed the street to the diner with a friendly greeting for people they met.

"What'll you have, boys?" They would always be boys to Alice. She had served them after school snacks for years and they continued to stop by often for the home style cooking.

Found By the Water

As they waited for their meals, Eric was unable to hide his enthusiasm. Josh asked, "Okay, what's this all about? I know it'll be good."

"I have an idea for persuading the valley that it isn't business as usual for Ceevwa." He used the local vernacular for the Chute Valley Water Authority (CVWA).

"I'm listening! Can't wait to hear your brainstorm."

"I've found the original fire department manuals." Eric repeated. "They maintained lower water levels deliberately so the valley has been dependent on your family for all these years."

Eric missed his friend's slight frown. "That's old news to me. I don't understand it either but tell me what you're thinking?"

"There's a close connection between Bellalto, CVWA and the fire department. My team can't do their jobs properly without a good water supply to back them up. I'd say the same is true in Chute Valley."

"I agree."

"This week I reviewed CVWA's policies and asked some questions. They don't have good relationships with valley leaders, so they don't have a true idea of the annual metered water needs. The lower region supplements with river water for firefighting. How could this still be going on?" Several heads turned at Eric's raised voice. "Josh, all I heard was the same old tales about valley versus mountain people."

"That's exactly why I stopped by this morning. To ask you to help turn things around. Do you have any ideas?" Josh gestured for Eric to lower his voice.

Eric leaned slightly forward over the table and adjusted his volume. "Yes. Quietly open the dam's headgates to allow for higher water in the lower Bella Chute. See if anyone notices. It'll be a good faith decision and show your sincerity." He ran his hand backwards over the top of his head. "What a hot summer! I've been worrying about their ability to fight a fire properly. The river is so low. In fact, I plan to visit the fire departments in the valley and review their water reserves. But first, let's raise the river below the dam."

"Let's text Dad now and tell him what you're suggesting." Josh typed something into his phone and waited a few seconds until his father replied. He handed the phone across the table. "You can explain it better than I can."

Found By the Water

"Okay, he said to go for it." Eric grinned a short time later. "He's going to meet me over there in ten minutes and we'll take care of this."

"I'll go with you and you can tell me more about updating the manuals. Are you still planning to take the ride with me to Marin next week?"

"Sure. Dani and I are meeting for lunch anyway so the timing is good. I'll drive."

Later, while relaxing on the patio, Josh realized how God had brought Eric into his life for such a time as this. Eric's ancestors had lived in the region for centuries before the settlers arrived. He cared about the natural resources and all the people who lived in the area. Josh was grateful that he and Eric trusted the same God. His friend, Dani Evans, was a gifted teacher. She had explained Jesus and the bible to Eric in a way that kept him looking for more. Eric had come to understand that God loved him without reservation. He was a praying man now. It made all the difference. Josh thought about the implications of Eric's plan. *'Opening the headgates is a great idea. Thank you, Lord, for my creative problem-solving friend.'*

Chapter 6

As much as depends on you, live peaceably. Romans 12:18

Feeling optimistic the next day, Josh called Anna again for an appointment. As the phone rang, he quickly reviewed what he knew about her. *'She is the town council,'* he thought, *'The rest will follow her lead.'*

"Hi, this is Joshua Marineta, Deputy Legal Counsel at CVWA, leaving another message for the Mayor. Anna, would you please return my call?"

It was clear he would have to reach her in person. But first he would try Glen Stuart, the Council Vice Chair. He maintained an office at the Town Hall related to his job as Marin's Building Inspector. He had seemed like a reasonable man the few times Josh had met him.

Sitting at her desk listening as Josh left his message, Anna frowned. He was the last person she wanted to talk to. Since her early years she had been hearing about them; how every bad thing that happened to Marin was due to a Marineta water decision.

"This guy isn't going away." Reinforcing her resolve, she said to herself, "But I won't give them a chance to do any more harm."

Anna began to rehearse all her grievances against his family, who were thought of in Marin as robber barons, cheats, and liars. The animosity had become so bad, that no one from either town would willingly drive through the other. They used the bypass road meant for vacationers.

❧

Unknown to Anna as she fumed, the phone rang in Glen's office. "Hallo, Glen Stuart here. It's your dime," came a gravelly voice through the phone.

Found By the Water

"Hello Glen, this is Josh Marineta, from over in Bellalto. How are you?"

Josh's greeting met with silence. "Glen, are you there?"

With a deep sigh, Glen stiffened in his chair. "Yeah, Josh. Give me a second." He walked over to shut his door so Anna would not overhear.

"Okay, I'm back. First, let me express my condolences to your family on your grandfather's passing. He was a hard businessman. I'm hoping your father will be different." said Glen in a neutral voice. "What can I do for you?"

"I admit my grandfather wasn't always the easiest person to get along with. It's what I'm calling about though."

"If you think your family can raise rates again, you'll have a fight on your hands!"

"No, that's not it. I would like to meet with your town council. I've tried reaching Anna a couple times. I was hoping you would be able to persuade her to call me." Josh stood up and turned toward the window. He wondered anew how such strife was possible in all this beauty.

"Not I." Glen replied. "I'm not very fond of Anna and I know when to stay out of her way. Besides, I'm not exactly unsympathetic to her actions. After all these years, what could you say to us that would make any difference? Anyway, I've got to run." Glancing at his watch, he was in a hurry to end the call. "Please don't call me again about it. My answer won't change."

'That could have gone better.' Josh thought as Glen cut the connection.

Chapter 7

Which of you does not sit down first and count the cost? Luke 14:28

Board members were arriving for the first Water Authority meeting since the funeral. "Good to see you again." Rob boomed out as he shook hands with Tom Pettrie, CVWA's Director of Accounting and Finance, and several others. Their faces told the story. Some were unhappy about what was coming. Others were hopeful or unbiased as they sat down around the oval conference table. Rob took his seat in the middle. Josh sat across from him. The secretary, one of the hopefuls, read the notes from the last board meeting and turned it over to Rob.

"Thank you for coming tonight. It's an honor to be leading this fine company." Rob began. "As you know, my father prepared and appointed me to be his successor. A Marineta has held this position since the Water Authority formed as a privately owned corporation. I accepted with a great sense of responsibility. My father did a fine job at the helm and I hope to follow his example in that way. I miss him very much."

He looked around the table and saw that some apprehension had left a few faces. Others were waiting.

"It's no secret that my father and I disagreed on some policies and practices. One way is how we administer agreements with Bellalto and the Chute Valley. I believe it is time to make some adjustments."

The uneasiness was back and even some anger. "Before I explain any further, I would like to hear what you have to say."

Tom spoke up quickly, tapping his pen on the table. "I can't believe you're still holding on to your misguided opinions that will undoubtedly impact the regional economy. Hospitality is our main industry in Bellalto. Water is what draws people here. Without it, even the valley would suffer. A lot of them depend peripherally on tourist trade. We can't spare a gallon. Let them find other ways to solve their problems."

Found By the Water

"Now wait a minute, Tom!" Irene Givens, interjected. As CVWA's Human Resource Director, she was known for keeping a cool head. "You are being incredibly self-centered and tunnel-visioned," she chided gently. "I know Bellalto's business is dependent on tourism, including your family's interests. But there may be other ways to keep our standard of living and help the others. We haven't heard what Rob is thinking."

Rob listened as others gave their opinions. There was no consensus. Human nature at its best and worst. Some wanting to protect what they had and others still open to hear more.

"I hear that personal finances are a big issue." Rob began again. "It's understandable to a degree. I want to remind you that Bellalto is prosperous. We have many creative people living here. I love this town. But I am not willing for other communities to continue to get poorer so we can keep getting richer." He paused for a moment. They leaned back in their chairs, absorbing the fact that he was unwavering in his purpose. "I've asked my son Josh to explain what we're thinking. He is back in Bellalto as the Authority's Deputy Legal Counsel and is well-qualified for it with his background in Regulatory Compliance. I've appointed him to replace my former position on the board and asked him to develop a plan that will help us continue to prosper along with our neighbors. Please welcome Josh as a member of our team."

Taking a deep breath, Josh stood up. It was hard for him to sit still while talking through something he was this passionate about. He started moving around, drawing on the energy to fuel his confidence. The others, looking at him warily, saw his friendly smile but focused on the determination in his eyes.

"Dad asked me to do my own research, then devise a strategy that will move us into the future." He stopped pacing for a moment, his eyes meeting those around the table. He liked to know the truth in a man or woman. For him, the eyes were telling.

"I've read all the meeting notes for the last five years and I'm aware that there are varying positions on the subject. There have been a lot of in-depth discussions among you formally and informally. You have strong opinions. I am very respectful of all the great things you have done." This was met with soft murmurs and nods of agreement. Some members straightened up and began to listen more intently.

Found By the Water

"The goal of my study was to form my own opinions, rather than blindly adopting those of Dad or Grandfather. My father has done nothing to influence my conclusions. I'll explain the results of my analysis first. Then I'll propose a high-level plan of action. Afterward, I'd like to hear your thoughts. We need to keep this discussion within this group until we reach the point where we're ready to make our decisions public."

"The first thing I noticed was that there have been very few valley representatives at our annual public forums. I'm wondering why this is."

"Secondly, I saw evidence of unprecedented growth when I reviewed the financial statements for the Water Authority and Bellalto. Growth is good. When I delved into the details though, I realized that the rate increases to some of the Valley's less prosperous towns were much higher than I would have expected for four years straight." Slight frowns appeared again around the table.

"My third observation is that the towns with the higher rates are those where animosity toward us has increased the most. I've read old newspaper articles and searched through my family archives. I've been hearing stories since I was a child. Many of the feuds, if we can call them what they really are, started when the original founders disagreed on something everyone alive today has forgotten about!"

"Finally, I am proposing that we intentionally seek out and improve our relationships with our customers. This could include meeting with each town council in the valley to outline our goals and listen to their grievances. Many of them are valid. Also, to invite each council to send representatives to our meetings and formally appoint some of them as board members. We need to better understand the impact of our decisions on all our customers and give them the opportunity to collaborate with us." With this last piece of information, Josh stood still and waited for the silence to do its work.

Chapter 8

Come, and let us reason together. Isaiah 1:18

Mark Thompson shot Tom a quick look for confirmation and blurted out in a huff, "That's not true!' Mark managed the finance team.

"Which of the three points is not true, Mark?" Josh's tone was friendly.

"The third. We work hard at being fair but the towns make it difficult."

"It sounds like you agree with me on the first two observations. Okay, that's good. How do they make it difficult for CVWA to be fair?" Deciding to hold the rest of his remarks for another time, Josh sat down. He had not expected to delve this deep into the issues so quickly.

"Yes, I agree on the other two points. Your grandfather was fully on board with how we make our decisions. You have no idea how hard this job is."

"I admit I've never done it. I know you have many challenges in carrying out your responsibilities. My distance from the details allows me to make impartial observations based on the facts presented in the financial reports. I mentioned them today so that you can help me understand how and why the towns make it difficult." Josh said in a quiet unassuming voice. Others observing the exchange saw Josh as kind and even tempered, unlike his late grandfather.

Tom entered the discussion. "Well, for one thing, the people who represent these towns will not engage with us. They dislike us so much they refuse to send their water usage forecasts and other reports that would help us determine reasonable rates. We charge what we think is appropriate per capita. And they get angrier. If we get it wrong and rates are higher than elsewhere, so be it. Josh, you know how bad it is. They've become insular."

Found By the Water

"I know it's bad, Tom. I wonder if anyone else has seen the same thing; how customer relationships and policies are based on rancor fostered over many years. Wouldn't it be more valuable to conduct our business with integrity and fairness?" Josh took a sip of water to give him time to approach the next sensitive subject. "I detect a little bit of greed on our part, too." With this quietly said, he turned to his father to gauge his reaction to the dynamics around the table. Josh now knew who the ringleaders were and what the silence of the other members meant. He had shaken up a few people. It was what he had intended to do without making enemies. He hoped they would want to move ahead with a higher standard. Suddenly, they all started talking over each other. Some were smiling and ready to leave the old ways behind. Some shook their heads in disagreement. Tom and Mark had leaned in toward each other talking rapidly, Mark's hands moving.

Rob clicked his pen against his water glass to get everyone's attention. The room quieted in an instant and they came to order again. This meeting was going exactly as he had thought it would. A deep acrimonious core had been gently prodded, and it had not been welcome.

'Most of us don't like our weaknesses to be publicly acknowledged,' he thought ruefully. *'We have to recognize it though so we can move ahead.'*

"Thank you, Josh." Rob said aloud, deciding not to go any further with the discussion. They needed time to absorb that changes were coming. "Your observations are in line with mine. I know the extent of your due diligence. We have determined that it started all those years before any of us were born. I'd like us all to consider if our need for the previous leaders' approval has affected our desire to do the right thing. Those leaders were my family. I make no excuses. They had many great strengths in business and as human beings. But they allowed generations of bitterness to cloud their judgment. I want to achieve a new era of leadership that serves all its customers equitably. It starts today."

He continued after pausing for emphasis. "I am asking each of you to choose if you are willing to address the issues with me and work together as a Board to create a new transformational way of doing business. Please let me know personally and in writing before the next meeting. You already realize it might cost us individually and corporately. Our way of life is enabled by income levels based on current policies. If you decide

Found By the Water

to resign from the Board, your positions within the company are not at risk unless you decide to work elsewhere. I hope you stay. I am certain there is a creative way to move forward. For now, if there are no other comments, we can move on to other agenda items. Irene, would you take the lead on the next one?"

The meeting ended amiably an hour later. Rob made sure he shook the hand of every board member before they left. When they were alone in the room, Rob clapped his son on the back. "A great job, Josh. It's what I expected of you. I knew your conclusions might differ from mine, instead you confirmed them. I want the others to start thinking for themselves as well. I hope everyone stays with us but if not, I'm prepared to deal with that."

"I was confident of my findings but not so much in the Board's reactions. I want our success to be unclouded by old animosities, result in good relationships with all our customers and to help them understand your plan for reconciliation."

"Join me for dinner?" Rob asked. "What do you feel like having tonight?" They walked out and were quiet again as the setting sun glowed with hope for better days coming. The groundwork had begun.

Chapter 9

He who is slow to anger is better than the mighty. Proverbs 16:32

Meg Stuart knew something was bothering her husband but getting him to talk about it was a whole other matter. Still, she had to try. She could not stand it when he shut her out. Married for twenty years, she knew him well. When he came in the house after cutting the grass, she watched him washing his hands, his back to her. She loved her slim, blond 48-year-old husband. "You know I'll get it out of you eventually, Glen. What's bothering you today?"

He gestured impatiently with his head. "Nothing, Meg darlin'. Just business."

Sighing, she slipped her arms around his waist. "It sometimes helps to share. You know I'm a good listener."

After a few seconds, Glen turned around to face his pretty wife who appeared much younger than her true age of forty-three years. Her chin length auburn hair and dusting of pale freckles highlighted her deep blue eyes. He put his arms around her and bent to kiss her lightly. "It's a water issue again. I wonder what life would be like without having that noose around our necks?"

"It's Anna, isn't it?" Meg exclaimed, forgetting her claim to be a good listener. "What's she up to now? I swear, there isn't a moment in time she isn't causing trouble. That woman wouldn't know how to be nice if her life depended on it!" Meg had never liked her. In Meg's opinion, she had grown up in a fancy house and gotten the best jobs because she was a Marin. "She acts like a town matriarch and she's my age. She breezed through life with ease."

"What? I said it was a *water* issue!" Glen replied mostly ignoring Meg's diatribe. But she saw the irritation in his eyes.

Found By the Water

"Josh Marineta called me today. He's been trying to reach Anna to discuss something. Since Mike is gone, I bet it has to do with the Water Authority. I didn't appreciate that he tried to use me to get to her. I told him no, a flat outright no. I cannot afford to cross her. Let him figure out how to connect with her on his own." Glen walked out of the kitchen to change for dinner.

While she put dinner on the table, Meg fumed about what she still thought of as an Anna issue. She had hoped that Glen would be in a good mood so she could broach her latest vacation idea. He was always more willing to spend money when not worried about losing his job. A smile and kind word, which rarely came from Anna, could work wonders on him. She knew enough to let it go for now and wait for a more opportune time. It was going to be hard enough later considering the council meeting was tonight. She wanted to talk to her friend Dani at bible study anyway. She had a knack for putting things into perspective.

Dinner was a quiet affair. Meg watched anxiously from the front window as Glen walked down the driveway on his way to the town hall, where he had left his car earlier in the day. His broad shoulders sagged a little on his well-sculpted frame.

Walking calmed Glen's nerves. He had not told his wife about his visit to his doctor today. *'Better to wait,'* he thought. *'See if it clears up on its own. The stress Anna adds to my life is not helping.'*

Chapter 10

He who heeds counsel is wise. Proverbs 12:15

When Glen arrived, he saw Anna and Brea talking in low tones. The other board members knew Brea sought status as Anna's protégé. *'I wonder what's going on now?'* Glen thought. Everyone found seats at the table, with Brea taking the closest to the right of Anna, who brought the meeting to order.

"Thank you for coming tonight." Anna began. "I've rearranged the agenda to talk about a looming issue. It is the only item up for discussion. We all know that Mike Marineta of CVWA died last month. Josh, his grandson, has been trying to reach me but we haven't connected yet. I don't know what they're up to but if its anything like all the other things that family has done, it's not good. I plan to drive a hard bargain the next time the rate renewals are due. We can't go on like this." Anna stopped to take a breath and a sip of water.

'Typical Anna,' Glen thought. *'She barrels right on with her own agenda without asking for anyone else's thoughts. Not this time, if I have anything to say about it.'* He quickly glanced around the room and saw from their expression's others were thinking the same thing. Only Brea wore a pleased expression.

"Excuse me Anna," Glen began. "If you don't know what Josh wants to talk about, how can you already have decided how to deal with him?" The others nodded.

"I don't need to hear him out to know the Marinetas are only interested in one thing. Money." Anna rapidly shot back at Glen.

"Maybe it would be a good idea to meet with him," Glen tenaciously continued. "I'm concerned about river levels. The department reservoir is low and it's not auto filling. It's hotter this summer than in other years.

Found By the Water

The river is lower than normal and the town is in danger." In addition to his other responsibilities, Glen was Marin's Fire Chief. He spoke from experience. He was worried.

Anna stood from her seat, looking annoyed that all the members were not falling in line with her. "Bellalto has been profiting off the backs of towns all over Chute Valley for generations. Mike was the worst of the lot. The water supply would dwindle back with the excuse of a drought, or aging equipment that needs replacing and then they would raise the rates. Water flow would improve for a while, then slowly go back down; so gradually we didn't notice until there would be another rate hike. The cycle repeats over and over. It amounts to extortion."

Glen raised his voice for emphasis. "We all know things need to change Anna! I want to hear what Josh has to say." He looked around the table. "Does anyone else want to meet with him? Can we put our anger aside for a short while to listen?" One by one others began to voice their opinions.

"Maybe we need to contact the state to see if they can stop the abuse," Sally Redmond offered.

Jacob Denver shook his head. "Old Man, um, Mike Marineta, had the commissioners in his pocket. They'll side with that family no matter what. The only way to move forward is to listen to what Josh has to say. Let's put our emotions and ill-feelings aside for now. We have an obligation to the town."

"The board is still made up of Marineta cronies from the hospitality industry in Bellalto. That's the bulk of the income in that area. Money talks, and the new kid sure isn't going to budge their opinions." Brea muttered loud enough to be heard. There were a couple nods of agreement around the table.

Glen spoke up. "I know Rob Marineta is well liked. The rumor is he and his father butted heads more than once. Some of the CVWA board are hoping that Rob's leadership will turn things in a new direction."

Brea spoke then, glancing at Anna for approval. "But *we* don't really know Josh, do we? What if he takes after his grandfather? He may be interested in padding his own pockets now that he has some authority over there. I agree with Anna. We can't trust him."

Found By the Water

"Have you ever met him?" Jacob asked quietly. "Do we even know what he looks like anymore? Why don't we give him a chance? Maybe he isn't anything like his grandfather."

Anna shook her head. "I know what I know about that family. Nothing will ever change."

"Is there anything else you want to add before we vote on it?" Anna asked. She met with silence. "Okay, all in favor of meeting with Josh, raise your right hand." Five hands went up. "All opposed, by the same sign." Three hands went up, including Anna's. Acquiescing, she continued. "Alright, I'll call Josh back and arrange a meeting with him." Disgruntled, she closed the meeting.

Council members filed out, not speaking until they were outside the building. No one noticed Brea hanging back with a sour look on her face. She turned around to find Anna and realized she had slipped out the back door.

Glen climbed into his car. He turned slightly to grab the seat belt and his eye caught movement on the building steps. It was Brea coming out again. Something about her expression gave Glen a sense of foreboding and put him instantly on alert. He climbed out of the car and stood waiting on the sidewalk for Brea to walk toward him on her way home. She was deep in thought.

"Good night Brea."

She gasped; hand pressed to her heart. "Glen, you startled me! I thought you'd be gone by now."

"Just leaving. Jacob and I had a few things to discuss and I'm a little late going home. As you are, Brea. I saw you come out with the rest of us a while ago."

Brea shifted her weight restlessly not meeting his gaze. "Some final touches on a report I'm working on." She explained vaguely. "Well, good night Glen. I'm heading home now. Have a nice evening." With that, she turned and walked away, her back rigid.

Glen mentally filed the moment away. '*I'll keep an eye on her.*' He drove away asking God for insight and turned his thoughts to a relaxing evening watching his favorite football team win.

❧

Found By the Water

Driving home, Anna mentally reviewed the discussion. *'I'll call Josh and I'll take my time about it. Lately, all I get is push back from everyone. But it's better not to say anything. I can't do my job without them. This burden of responsibility is too much for me sometimes.'*

Chapter 11

Let us not grow weary while doing good. Galatians 6:9

Sitting in his office a week later, Josh Marineta wondered if he should make the drive to Marin and surprise Anna at the town hall. He could invite her to have lunch with him at the lake so they could talk in neutral territory. Fed by many streams running off the river, Lake Chute was a popular vacation spot with a well-maintained beach. Mountain towns in the area worked hard to welcome visitors. Josh thought about the contrast between Bellalto and Marin. If he remembered correctly, Marin had a tired look and nothing there attracted visitors.

In contrast, Bellalto depended on tourism. When the last of the warm weather crowds left, locals had a month or two to catch their breath before the next wave flowed in. They were proud of the main business area with its shops and restaurants. Bed and breakfasts and small family-owned inns filled up quickly all year round. Everyone worked hard to create a memorable experience for their guests. The Mountain Lodge built higher up near the magnificent waterfall, was the largest hotel of its kind in the area. There were no chain accommodations because it would ruin the charming image Bellalto fostered.

He pulled himself back to the challenging task of connecting with the Mayor. Nothing would change until he did.

"If I'm going to do this today, I'd better get going." He said aloud. His phone rang as he reached for it.

"Hello? I'd like to speak with Joshua Marineta, please." The woman said crisply.

"You're in luck. This is Josh." He said warmly.

"Josh, this is Anna Marin. I'm returning your calls. It has taken a while for me to get back to you. Thank you for your patience."

Found By the Water

"Anna! I am so glad to finally speak with you. I would like to talk to you and the council about some new ideas to improve Marin's relationship with the Chute Valley Water Authority. Could we arrange a time to meet in person?"

There was a lengthy pause. "Anna?"

"Josh, are these ideas related to raising the water rates again? Because by my calendar, annual rate changes are not due for another three months. When the time comes, I think you'll find that we will drive a harder bargain this year. We'll no longer be pushed around."

"Some of what I'd like to discuss is related to current rate levels but there is much more. You must have heard that my grandfather died recently." He paused a second and continued when Anna did not offer the customary condolences. "My father has taken the helm at the Water Authority. He's different than Grandfather in many ways. We have been working on how to change our relationships with valley customers. I want to explain and hear the council's input. Are you willing to meet with me first?"

"I'm not convinced it is a good idea but the council discussed this at our last meeting and we voted to meet with you to hear you out. I'm not available until next week. Let's say Tuesday, 5:00 pm, in my office before the meeting?"

Realizing he was not going to get much more from her then, he decided to hold the offer of lunch until he arrived for the meeting.

Chapter 12

If you knew who it is who says to you, give me a drink. John 4:10

The following Monday morning Josh turned to his friend with a grin. "I know you prefer the bypass to get to Dani's house. Thanks for agreeing to go through town this time so I can see something of Marin first." He had reserved two rooms at a small inn on the far side of Marin. By going a day early, he could walk around town before the meeting.

"No problem, buddy." Eric said, as he concentrated on driving. "Since I'm in a hurry to get to Dani's, I'll drop you off at the inn and check in later." Smiling to himself, Josh nodded his head. "You're always in a hurry. Fine with me. It will take as long as it takes." He knew how important the outcome of this visit was. "Greed on one side, anger on the other has simmered for far too long. It is time for reconciliation."

Suddenly, they heard a knocking and a click-click under the hood, then silence. Eric reacted quickly, and the car coasted to a stop well on to the shoulder of the road. Frustration poured out of him as he tried engaging the ignition. "You must be kidding me! This can't be happening!"

"There's no service either." Josh put his phone away. "I'll walk into town and send assistance back to you."

"That's crazy. It's a good five miles and it's the hottest day of the year!"

"I'll be fine," Josh said, grabbing a bottle of Bella Aqua from the back seat. "Settle in and get comfortable. I'll see you in a bit."

Two hours later, Josh saw the outline of the town. A sign said, 'Welcome to MARIN.' He entered a residential area with no service station in sight. With phone service available, he tried calling Eric but the phone battery had died on the walk in. *'This is exasperating. Everything I've tried to do is delayed for one reason or another. What else will happen today? I should have had a contingency plan.'*

Found By the Water

He bent his tall frame and gratefully sat down on the porch steps of the first house he came upon. *'Not a moment too soon,'* he thought. He ran his forearm across his forehead. "The area is as parched as I feel," he said aloud while scanning the surrounding countryside.

"It's hot and dry, I agree. How can I help you?" He turned at the sound of the voice and recognized Anna Marin coming around the south corner of the house. She was an attractive woman whose age was difficult to tell. He could see that life had been hard for her. He stood and took a step forward to greet her properly. She tilted her head up slightly to stay engaged. Her gray eyes were defensive.

"Why are you sitting on my porch?" she continued with a short jerk of her hand for emphasis. She gave a small toss of her head toward the porch that caused her chin length hair to swing slightly.

"My friend and I were on our way to Marin and his car broke down about five miles out. We couldn't get a signal to call for service so he stayed with the car. I walked into town to get help."

"Does this look like a service station?" She stood with one hip cocked and hands on her waist. A small smile fleetingly appeared.

"No, but it looks like a nice shady place to rest before moving on." He turned his full smile on her. "I only sat down a moment ago. I didn't think you'd mind." Anna noticed that when he smiled, an inner light radiated from him with a staggering force. Inexplicably drawn in, her stance became a little less wary.

"Could I trouble you for some cold water, please? It's a hot day for the long walk I've had."

Her eyes narrowed. "You came in this way? Do you live in Bellalto?"

"Yes, ma'am. I do."

"You came from Bellalto and you ask me for a drink?" She asked incredulously. Looking deliberately at the empty water bottle with its incriminating logo, he had set on the step near him, she raised an eyebrow.

Josh looked at her with compassion and quietly said, "If you knew who I am you'd ask for all the water you can ever drink."

Annoyed she replied, "Wait! I know who you are now. You're Josh Marineta, aren't you? You're a day early."

"Yes, I am. I have been trying to introduce myself. Anna? It's great to finally meet you." He held out his hand in greeting. "It looks like your lovely gardens could use some water too."

Found By the Water

She shook his hand. "Well, Josh, this isn't how I envisioned meeting you." She opened her mouth to give him a piece of her mind, then his lovely garden remark registered. She softened her voice slightly. "Our meeting isn't until tomorrow. What are you doing here?"

"I came a day early so I could look around and get to know the town a little better. I hope you don't mind. I haven't been through Marin in a long time."

"I see." Anna walked up the steps and into her home. A few minutes later, she handed him a small glass of cold water and sat down two steps above him, to his left. He had to turn to see her. "This is all I can offer you right now. Come back in a couple of days if you want more. Are you aware of how Marin has suffered from your family's practices? We barely have enough water each month to live on. It's been this way for longer than my lifetime. It's worse this summer than most."

He gratefully took a long cool swallow. "I know. It's why I came. I hope to fix the situation with your help. But my friend has waited long enough with the car and I've already intruded on your day. Would you mind leaving that discussion for tomorrow as planned? I would appreciate it if I could use your phone to call for roadside aid. My battery died on the walk into town."

Relieved to have time to gather her thoughts before the meeting, Anna replied, "I'll grab my car keys and drive you over to Will's. He's the most qualified mechanic in town and he's honest. He'll give you the best service and I'll make sure he does it for a reasonable price."

As they drove to Mackey's Garage, they were both quiet. Their first meeting had occurred differently than planned. The surprise introduction had changed the dynamics.

Chapter 13

Seek the peace of the city and pray. Jeremiah 29:7

Will Mackey was a friendly, pleasant man. He asked some questions to determine the nature of the repair, loaded some tools into his truck, grabbed some cold bottled water and said to Josh, "Hop in." Anna gave a brief wave and headed back home. A short while later, they were at the car handing Eric the water. Will was able to repair the car on the spot.

"What are you fellas doing driving through town?" He asked. "Most folks take the bypass."

"I'm Josh Marineta and this is my good friend, Eric Miller. We're coming from Bellalto. I have some business interests in town." Josh replied.

"How do you know the Mayor? Seems you caught her on a good day. Most days it's like walking on eggshells around her." Will wiped his hands before he climbed into his truck. Leaning his elbow through the open window, he paused. "Wait. You're a Marineta?" He grunted. "The bypass would have been a better choice." His friendliness cooled considerably.

"We met today for the first time. I landed on her porch to rest after the long hot walk. After the surprise of seeing a stranger sitting on her porch, she was reasonable. Even offered to drive me to your garage, Will. Thank you for all your help. Hope we meet again." Josh paid him and they were on the road again heading into Marin.

When they arrived at the inn, Eric called Dani to rearrange lunch to an early dinner. She offered to pick him up so she could stop at a building site on the way. Dani Evans was the sole proprietor of Evans Construction. She had relocated to Marin four years earlier after completing some tourism related projects in the area.

Found By the Water

She had learned from the best at her father's side working in Midwest states where she had grown up. Acceptance on her own merits was important to her. The region's potential for growth was appealing and Marin's cost of living was attractive, so she bought a small house and moved her business. Now thirty-two years old, she had first met Eric when he came to inspect one of her Bellalto building sites. It was her long black hair and confident manner that had first attracted Eric's attention. In the end, her forthright manner and kindness had drawn him in. They had been dating for a few months.

"Why are you staying in town tonight, Eric?" Dani asked when they were at their table. The restaurant was one of their favorites. The lake reflected the surrounding mountains. An expanse of blue calm, it sparkled with the last of the day's sunshine. It was early enough for boats to still be on the water.

"I drove Josh in for a meeting tomorrow morning with Anna Marin. He's intent on getting to know her and the town council on behalf of the Water Authority."

"I heard about that meeting. My friend, Meg, is married to Glen Stuart. He's Anna's Vice-Chair and the Fire Chief. You might have met him professionally as he's also Marin's building inspector. Meg dislikes Anna although I'm not sure of her reasons. I'll pray the meeting goes well. We need better relationships with the Marineta family. I hope Anna will realize it too." Dani said.

"If anyone can get through to Anna, it's Josh. Why don't we order and relax? I want to hear about your bible study. I'd like to join you sometime. I have so much to learn. If you like, we can take a ride around the lake after dinner." When the waiter had taken their menus and stepped away with their choices, Eric said. "First, tell me about your latest project."

❧

Josh spent Monday evening walking around Marin. The homes were neat and cared for, without being showy. A few people stopped their evening yard work to greet him. They were curious. It was rare to see a stranger walk by. At the mention of the Water Authority their friendly overtures cooled, like Will's had. Some raised their eyebrows in surprise, others made polite excuses and turned away. Even so, he was glad he had decided to come early. He knew now for certain it wasn't only Anna he had to influence for good. It was an entire town.

Found By the Water

Back at the inn, he again turned to God for wisdom. "A soft answer turns away wrath." He read aloud from his bible. "But a harsh word stirs up anger."[2] He fell asleep affirming his trust in God and slept so soundly that he did not hear the lightening as it struck some place close, shortly past midnight.

&✑

As Brea pulled into her driveway, she saw a tall man walk by. Behind him, her neighbors were gathering in small groups. She joined the closest. "Hi. What's going on?"

"That man walking around the neighborhood? He's Josh Marineta. You know, of the Water Authority family." Her neighbor replied.

"What's he doing in Marin?" Brea asked with a slight frown.

"Has a meeting tomorrow with the Mayor. It can't be good for us."

"Why is he walking around town a day before the meeting?" Brea asked under her breath.

Her neighbor heard her. "Good question. No one dared ask him. If you hear anything, let me know."

The group broke up and returned to their homes. Brea sat down with a soda to think through what this new development meant. *'I can keep an eye on him tomorrow. Before the interview at the Farin', I'll wander over to Main Street for a while. It might help my chances of getting hired at the paper if I can bring in some newsworthy items.'* She thought.

'How's Marin Faring?' was the official name of Marin's small-town newspaper. Locals referred to it as the Farin'. It was mostly news related to local business and events, new families who had moved to town, family reunions, and the usual word puzzles and jokes. When Brea had decided to look for other work to supplement her rafting income, she saw the ad for an op-ed page editor. She had gained experience working on a military base newspaper and it would be perfect for her purpose. *'This is the key to my strategy. I'll have first-hand access to local opinions about Marin and can decide which to print. It'll be useful in disrupting whatever the Marinetas have up their sleeves. Maybe Sean will take more notice of me.'*

Chapter 14

When you walk through the fire, you will not be burned. Isaiah 43:2

The next afternoon, Glen shut down his computer and straightened his desk. He sent a text to his wife, stretching to work out the tension in his back from sitting for hours. '*Leaving work now. Be there in ten. Need anything?*' As he walked to his car, his cell phone sounded with a siren, his fire department ring tone. He answered urgently, "Talk to me!"

"Chief, have a hot fire on Main! The diner. We're half capacity, with tankers low on water and crew on vacation. Not enough water." Lieutenant Handley informed him in rapidly delivered staccato. "Calling in mutual aid." Glen knew the back-up towns were closer to the river than Marin but it would still take a while to arrive. "River level's up some. Can reload directly from it. Have your turnout gear."

Glen ran a hand through his hair in frustration. "I'll meet you there." He speed-dialed home. "Change of plans. Fire at the diner."

Meg's brief answer was, "Praying. Bye."

He heard a clap of thunder. All he could see was the clear blue sky above the sunset. '*Dry heat storm, most likely,*' he thought. The sky was darker off in the distance to the north.

Jogging to his car, he jumped in, popped on the small light strobe, and jammed the car into gear. He sped to the scene and parked as close as he could get. A small crowd of on-lookers stood well behind the safety protocols in place. The Lieutenant ran up to him with his gear. "Chief." he greeted Glen with a nod of respect. As Glen suited up, he barked, "Update!"

"Diner closed at 2:00 pm. The Bolton's are out of town. Alarm went off at 3:45 pm. Didn't you hear it? Team completed the primary search. No one trapped to our knowledge."

Found By the Water

Glen saw major smoke and knew it had smoldered in the walls for a long time before setting off the alarm. There was a loud explosion. He watched as shock waves blew out windows and walls on one side. The dining room disappeared, engulfed. Flames shot outward in all directions, licking exteriors of the adjacent buildings. A murmur rose from the onlookers as they shifted quickly backward.

"Aim the hoses to the secondary blaze! Get foam on the electrical source!" Glen ordered. The whole block was at risk for conflagration. "Call the gas company and have them cut the supply to this entire area. NOW!" Glen directed his men. *'This is a mess,'* he thought and hoped they had enough water to keep the blaze from spreading. Over at the edge of the cordoned off area Glen spotted an ambulance with paramedics standing by. He offered up a silent prayer. *'Please, Lord. Don't let us need them today!'*

Chapter 15

A heart that devises wicked plans. Proverbs 6:18

Josh walked toward the town hall for his meeting with Anna. The sight and smell of smoke quickened his pace. He rounded the corner onto Main Street and flinched. The heat hit him with force. Josh watched the scene with dread as the fire burst out of control. Recognizing the Fire Chief as Glen Stuart, Josh approached him.

"You're getting more resources on this? I'd like to help!" he yelled to Glen over the roar of the flames and hoses.

Glen fixed a penetrating gaze on Josh. Weary, pale, and rubbing his chest as if he had indigestion, Glen answered, "Other crews are coming. Would Bellalto Fire assist?"

Josh grabbed his cell phone and spoke rapidly. "Eric! MFD needs mutual aid response from Bellalto for a multi-alarm fire on Main Street. Call it in, will you? Raise the headgates again, too." He listened, nodding his head. "Okay. Get it done. Thanks." He turned back to Glen. "More help is coming. I'm on my way to meet Anna." Glen nodded as he focused on the blaze. Josh spun around and ran to the town hall. Glen fleetingly registered *'raise the headgates again.'*

Anna was trying unsuccessfully to reach the owners of the diner. She crossed her arms while Josh brought her up to date on the fire containment and his requests to Eric. She asked with eyes narrowed. "What will you charge us for the extra?"

Josh leveled a look back at her. "Accept it as the gift it is," his voice curt.

Anna stood and walked from behind the desk to face him. She continued, "I want to believe that."

She moved quickly toward the door. "I have a lot of questions for Rob. Right now, I have to see how things are going over on Main."

Found By the Water

It was worse than Anna had expected. There were tongues of flame reaching through the roof and all sides of the diner, though the walls of adjacent buildings were not burning yet. Several tankers from area townships were hosing them down. As one tanker emptied, the drivers would move out of position to fill-up and a full one would take its place. Firefighters in full protective gear went in and out of the fiery building, directing streams of water, and made sure no one was inside. Watching Glen in the thick of the effort coordinating all the fire companies to function as one united force, Anna stiffened suddenly, moving closer to catch Glen's attention. She gestured toward the diner. He nodded and spoke to some of his men, who hurried away. Finally, the diner was only a pile of embers that sent a black plume upward and drifting through the town center. The fire was contained at last.

❧

Standing to the side of the crowd behind the safety zone perimeter, Brea was close enough to observe Anna's panicked interaction with Glen. No one noticed her standing there. An idea began to form. Turning away toward the Farin' office, she smiled to herself.

Chapter 16

God is the strength of my heart. Psalm 73:26

The other fire companies were pulling out one by one as Glen released them from duty. He personally shook everyone's hand before they left, including Eric's, who had donned gear and worked alongside for hours. He turned and walked toward Josh and Anna. Eric had already joined them. They noticed how tired and pale he looked beneath the soot on his face.

He extended his hand to Josh and nodded at Eric. "Thank you for raising the water level in the river. We couldn't have avoided losing additional structures without it. The backdraft from the windows blowing out could have signaled disaster for us. The Lord brought you here with perfect timing. No life-threatening injuries; some minor burns and a little smoke inhalation."

He turned to Anna, catching a glimpse of Brea moving furtively away from the crowd. "You should head home, Anna. Things are under control now. We'll watch the site for the rest of the night to make sure it doesn't reignite. I'll see you in the morning to write the official re-," he suddenly groaned and grabbed his chest. Josh quickly caught and lowered him to the ground as Glen stumbled back a few steps, legs buckling. "I can't breathe!" he gasped. "My chest hurts!"

"Help! The Chief collapsed!" Josh yelled. Without a second's hesitation, the emergency workers grabbed their equipment and rushed to Glen's side. One tore open Glen's clothes to expose his chest and attach a cardiac monitor. Another applied oxygen and started an intravenous line in his arm.

Anna watched in horror as Josh quietly asked, "Do you have his wife's number in your phone? She needs to be notified."

Found By the Water

"No." She replied. "I-I only ever contact him about council business. I never thought to ask for Meg's."

Lieutenant Handley said, "I'll call Meg, let her know what's happening." He walked away to make the call.

Sweating and pale, Glen's hand went to his chest. "Please, someone, pray for me!" Josh knelt beside him and reached for his hand, careful not to disturb the paramedics.

"Jesus, we ask for your intervention in Glen's life right now. Give him and Meg peace. Amen."

"Thanks," Glen said weakly. Motioning for Anna to come closer he whispered, "Brea. Watch-" he groaned and went still.

"He's in V-Tach," the paramedic with the heart monitor yelled.

"No pulse, no breathing," another answered. "Starting compressions!"

Organized chaos ensued as the team reacted. The team leader called dispatch for an emergency medivac helicopter, another attached defibrillator pads to Glen's chest after drying off the sweat. Someone placed a resuscitator bag mask over Glen's face and began to give him breaths in a steady rhythm.

"Shock advised! Charging to 200. All clear!" The team fell back, no one touching the man struggling with life. As the cardiac monitor alarmed, the operator yelled "All clear. Shocking!" After a quick scan all around, he pushed a button and Glen's body jerked. CPR resumed until Glen started struggling. "Hold CPR!" the team leader said. "Vitals!"

"I've got a pulse, sinus tach at 110, BP 90 with 90 over 50, respirations 14."

"You with us, Glen?" the leader asked. Glen moaned and nodded. "We'll monitor and support him until medical transport arrives." He said to Anna, "Glen will be transported to Valley General Hospital. Someone needs to get his wife there ASAP."

They heard an approaching helicopter overhead. A landing zone quickly cleared in the middle of Main Street. Anna and Josh each drew a deep breath and watched as they loaded Glen onto a stretcher and into the helicopter. They watched silently as the lights of the helicopter disappeared into the night.

Chapter 17

Bear one another's burdens. Galatians 6:2

Anna acknowledged the Bellalto contingent before leaving the scene of the fire. "Thank you, gentlemen, for all you did today. I'm heading home to make some more phone calls. Josh, I'll call you in a few days to reschedule our meeting." As she walked, Anna became aware that her heart was racing. "Anxiety," she acknowledged quietly to herself. She did not notice how the neighbors stepped back to clear a path or how carefully they watched her. None of them would have known the turmoil going on inside by her expression. Some of them started to follow at a distance as she turned the corner on to her street.

'It's devastating,' she thought. *'I was useless today!'*

"Anna! Anna, wait up," her reverie interrupted. She turned and saw Josh jogging up behind her.

"What is it, Josh?" She replied quietly. "Whatever it is, can it wait? I'm done in. I want to get to the hospital to find out how Glen is doing."

"Anna, I'd be happy to come with you." Shaking her head, she turned toward the house. As she reached the steps, her neighbor Bob walked across the lawn to confront her.

"Really, Mayor? Things in this town can't be much worse economically and you're going home after the fire destroyed the Bolton's livelihood?" Disbelief in his voice. "What are you planning to do about the water scarcity? We've had enough of this." He turned to give Josh a pointed look. Word had gotten around fast.

"Bob, this is not the time." Distracted by the people gathering on the sidewalk waiting for her response, she stopped talking. She opened her mouth to continue but it was no use. She walked into the house and leaned on the other side of the door with her eyes closed, breathing deeply.

Found By the Water

"Maybe it's not such a good idea to go to the hospital tonight. I should probably wait until the morning." She said aloud to her empty house and picked up her phone to call instead.

"Hello? ER? This is Anna, the Mayor over in Marin. I'm calling about my Fire Chief, Glen Stuart, who's on his way to you tonight. Can you tell me if he arrived?" She paused to listen. "Oh, Okay. I was hoping you'd have more information than that to tell me. Sure, okay. I'll drive over in the morning."

The doorbell pealed as she ended the call. "Now what?" Anna said opening the door. Not recognizing the man standing there, she stood silently waiting for him to speak first.

"Anna, I'm Eric Miller," he said, reaching out a hand to greet her. "I'm Fire Chief over in Bellalto and a friend of Josh Marineta. I was in fire gear when we met earlier. I wanted to give you some peace of mind tonight. I introduced myself to your firefighters and was working the fire with them. I didn't have a chance to talk to you before you left. A neighbor told me where you live. I'll be staying with your crew tonight to make sure the fire doesn't reignite. We'll refill the tankers from the river and have them ready in case of a flare up. Is there anything else I can do for you tonight?"

Stunned at the unfamiliar solicitude for her, Anna gazed at Eric for a few seconds. "It's nice to meet you, Eric. Thank you for your help tonight. I didn't recognize you. Would you like to come in for a few minutes? I have a lot on my mind. I guess I don't want to be alone as much as I thought. I'd usually ask Glen but, well, I'd appreciate it if you could spend a few minutes with me."

"Sure." Eric stepped into the foyer. He followed her into the living room. "Eric, please, have a seat," pointing to a side chair by the fireplace. "Would you like a cold soda while we talk?"

"Yes! Thanks." To Eric, the room was nice but seemed unused. *'Where was the rest of the town council? Surely there would be much to discuss.'*

Returning, she handed Eric the soda and sat on the other side of the fireplace. "I don't know how I'm going to tell the Bolton's. The diner is a special place in Marin. Could we have saved it if the tankers had been ready? We lost a lot of time waiting for enough water."

"I know about special diners. I imagine every town has one. What I saw was a fast, hot fire. I'm sure there will be an investigation when it

Found By the Water

cools enough but from what I understand, it may have been smoldering undetected for too long."

"I had no idea that the department water reserves were so low, although it makes sense since the river levels are. The department's reserve well has an automatic fill gauge linked with a pumping system from the river." She looked straight at him in defiance. "It saves us from paying for metered water." When there was no recrimination from Eric, she continued.

"But now that I'm thinking about it, the river has been too low for the auto-fill to engage." Her hands clenched in her lap. "It could have been much worse without you and your team stepping in. Thank you. How were you able to react so quickly?"

"That would be Josh's doing," Eric smiled. "I've known him most of my life. He's the man you want on your side."

"Josh. He's been trying to meet with me but I haven't been very accommodating. In this town, the Marinetas are not friends. What is it about Josh? He won't give up."

"Josh and Rob are good people. I have seen them in some tight places, willing to work with opposing parties because they want to change the way things have been. They want the whole region to prosper, not just the mountain economy. There are many people in Bellalto who disagree with them but they have strong convictions. What do you think of their plan?"

"I don't know what their plan is. I haven't wanted to hear it."

"You need to give him a chance. You saw tonight how much is at stake for Marin."

Anna jumped in her seat as the phone rang. "Excuse me. It's going to be a long night. Hello? Gus! I've been trying to reach you. It's not good news. Oh, you heard already. What? Yes, we can talk tomorrow. I'm going to the hospital in the morning to check on Glen, but after that, let's meet in my office. Okay. Yes, I know things need to change. Is your insurance current? Well, we'll work to get you back in business, I promise you. See you tomorrow. Drive safe." She sat down, absorbed in her thoughts.

"The thing is, Eric, I don't know where to start. I'm all alone in this town. I'm not even sure if I'm going to stay in Marin."

"Anna, you have a friend in Josh. You just don't know it yet. Mind if I pray with you before I leave? It sounds like you need God's help."

Found By the Water

Silent for a moment, she nodded. "I'm not a religious person. Lately, I've been wondering whether God could care about someone like me. My life hasn't been the most upright. I've had some tough breaks, too." She hesitated before asking, "Josh prayed tonight for Glen. What do you think happens when you talk to God? I've never known God to take much interest in me."

"I used to think like you. My parents traveled a lot and didn't have as much time with me as I needed. Josh and Rob filled the gap. They helped me understand that God loves me. It took a long time but the truth finally got through. I believe it. He loves you. I am sure of it. Anna, if he loves me, why wouldn't he care about you? Let's ask him to show you his love and how to work through the tough days you all have ahead of you. He hears our prayers."

"I'd like that although I don't believe. It feels like I'm in the deep end right now. Any help is welcome." She replied before Eric asked in a simple everyday way that God would reveal his love to Anna and help her to lead the town council through the weeks ahead. "I'll stop by again," he said as he took his leave.

Later, right before her eyes closed that night, Anna softly asked, "Could it be true God? You love me?"

❦

At that moment on a sidewalk near the inn, heaven heard another prayer. "God, This is unbelievably disappointing just when we're on the cusp of making things better. I'm depending on you to help us see our way through this mess. Show yourself to Anna and the others who live here. They need to know your love and power. I trust you to lead us."

He had not known Anna was so alone and hopeless. Tonight, there had been no sign of the confident in-charge person she had presented the other times. Then he walked by a church. The sign on the front lawn read, "For My thoughts are not your thoughts, nor are your ways My ways."[3] *'That's for sure'*, he thought. Taking out his phone, he dialed. "Eric, where did you go tonight? Hey, can you get a ride home with Dani so I can use your car to stop at the hospital tomorrow? Thanks for today. I owe you one."

Chapter 18

When they are in the land of their enemies, I will not cast them away.
Leviticus 26:44

Meg ended the call with the hospital. She sat at her kitchen table stunned and shaking. *'Doesn't make sense,'* was her first coherent, if cryptic thought. *'He's fit. Healthy. Only forty-eight. Runs every day. A heart attack? How had it not been known earlier he was at risk?'*

She numbly stared at nothing. "Lord, help!" was all she managed. The doorbell rang; then urgently a second time. Startled and on autopilot, Meg opened the door allowing her close friend and confidant to rush in.

"I came as quickly as I could." Dani said, hugging her tightly. "I can take you to the hospital. You don't look like you're in any condition to drive yourself."

"Yes." Meg's voice trembled slightly. She spoke over her shoulder rushing out of the room to dress. "I'm too shaky. It'll take me a few minutes to get ready. The lieutenant said they took him to Valley General."

Dani, with the familiarity of a close friend, took some travel mugs and made coffee. By the time Meg returned, she had two large coffees-to-go ready and waiting. She handed Meg one. "All set?"

"All set. Let's go." Meg swung her handbag to her shoulder and strode out the door.

She tried to relax and pray during the drive. "Dani," she asked quietly. "Why am I having trouble praying? All I can think of is what if he-," she broke off with tears in her eyes. "How could God allow this to happen? Glen's a good man. The kids and I...at a loss without him." Stumbling over her words, she continued. "Made the fire department and Council...by keeping things sane. Anna...run roughshod over if he... she's a tyrant! I get so mad!"

Found By the Water

"We are all on edge in the heat and drought, Meg," Dani said, ignoring for the moment her remarks about Anna." And from what I heard, it was a vigorous fire; touch and go for a while. It's natural you'd be anxious and find it hard to pray. The Holy Spirit is praying as he does when we can't find the words. He prays perfectly.[4] Who could be a better prayer partner than he? I'll pray too. Why don't you close your eyes and rest? You can agree without saying anything."

Meg nodded. Dani asked God to heal Glen; to give peace and wisdom to everyone involved. Meg was able to echo Dani's prayers silently. She calmed down by the time they reached the hospital.

Dani dropped Meg off at the main entrance of Valley General Hospital. The front desk directed her to the cardiac catheterization laboratory waiting room. She was pacing impatiently when Dani joined her.

A local all-news channel aired on the muted television. Footage of the fire played repeatedly. Cameras followed Glen's actions capturing him in constant motion. She occasionally caught site of Anna in the background and Brea standing behind her on the other side of the safety barrier. She blew out an irritated breath.

"He looks exhausted. I wonder where she is now, as he fights for his life! Somehow I know she's the reason he's here in the middle of the night." she muttered to herself.

Meg alternated between worry over Glen and irrational anger at Anna. She needed to blame someone. Her long-standing antagonism made Anna the focus of Meg's wrath. Finally, two women dressed in green scrubs, briskly entered the waiting room.

"Mrs. Stuart?" the younger woman asked, extending her hand. "I'm Dr. Janice Shapiro, the cardiologist on call tonight. Your husband has been in my care since they brought him in. Let me first assure you he is stable, albeit in profoundly serious condition. Let's sit while we talk."

"How is Glen?" Meg immediately asked. "All I know is he collapsed at the scene of the fire, needing CPR, and was flown here."

"He had a type of abnormal heart rhythm that essentially stopped it from beating and had to be shocked to reset it. Thankfully, they did it quickly." Dr Shapiro explained. "His heart resumed beating in normal rhythm and he regained consciousness before the flight. He had a myocardial infarction or an acute heart attack, as you would call it. I opened the blocked coronary artery and placed a stent in it to keep it open.

Found By the Water

He's pain-free now and his vital signs are good. We'll keep him in the Coronary ICU for a day or two so we can check him closely. There will be new medications and some lifestyle changes may be recommended."

Meg drew in a breath. "I had no idea he was at risk for this. He's so young. I don't understand how this could happen."

"Well, actually, I am wondering that myself." the cardiologist said. "The artery or blood vessel was only 50% partially occluded, or blocked, and that should not have caused the attack in and of itself. Has he been under undue stress lately? A stress reaction could cause coronary artery spasm. That combined with the narrowing of the blood vessel could cause total occlusion; to close up."

"More stress than the fire?" Meg asked.

"Ongoing stress over time raises the cortisol levels in the blood. Is he living with that kind of pressure day to day?" Dr. Shapiro answered. Meg considered for a moment. Her mind immediately turned to Anna before she told the doctor, "Glen has been under stress with his job and service on the town council. Recently, he's been dealing with conflict during the meetings."

"That explains a lot. Before he's discharged in a few weeks, we'll need to discuss relaxation techniques to help him. You can see him briefly in CICU now, then he has to rest." The doctor rose, shook Meg's hand, and left. The gray-haired woman with a motherly expression stood and smiled at Meg. "My name is Kathy. I am one of the nurses who works in the Cath Lab. I will take you to Glen. Come with me." She led the way to the elevator where they rode to the Intensive Care Unit and into his room. There was a heart monitor above the bed attached to Glen. An IV-line dripped fluid into his arm and oxygen flowed into his nose. Glen lay unmoving, eyes closed and pale. Another nurse stood by his side quietly typing on a computer. He stirred and opened his eyes when Meg took his hand.

"Hey you." Meg whispered, shaken by how weak he was. The monitors and strange sounds were intimidating. "How do you feel?"

Glen licked his dry lips and smiled a little. "Like I got run over by a truck! They say I'm doing okay, given the circumstances. I'm glad you're here."

Meg struggled with the tears that came and squeezed her husband's hand. "I love you! You're going to be fine!" She pulled up a chair and they held hands until Glen's eyes drooped shut and his breathing evened out. The nurse beckoned her to leave the room and led the way to the private waiting room where Dani was seated. They moved to two isolated chairs in the back. Meg quietly relayed the doctor's prognosis.

"The blockage wasn't large enough to cause the heart attack by itself. She said prolonged stress made the artery spasm and block completely off. This is Anna's fault! Glen has been on edge for months, easing tensions and arguments with her and others."

Dani made an ambiguous sound. Taking Meg's hand, she told her friend, "Let's give the situation to the Lord again while we wait."

Three hours later, Meg woke from a nap to the smell of fresh coffee. Dani handed her a steaming cup. "Here you go, sweetie. Thought you might need this."

Meg gratefully accepted it and inhaled the rich fresh brewed aroma. Sunlight shone through the window. "Thank you! What time is it?"

"About 10:30 am. It was a long night."

She took the first sip as Anna appeared in the waiting room entrance. She walked over smiling and awkwardly stood in front of the two tired women. "Good morning. How is Glen? I hope he is okay."

Stunned to see the focus of her anger in front of her, Meg stood so abruptly her coffee splashed on her shoes. "What are you doing here?" she demanded harshly. "This is your fault!"

Stunned by the outburst, her eyes widening, Anna froze. "I was there when Glen collapsed. I was worried about him."

"You don't know what it means to be concerned about someone else! You only care about yourself. You've brow-beaten the council to the point that Glen dreads every meeting. He takes on the peacemaker role. See where it got him? You've always been this way. I want you to leave. Now! Don't come back. You aren't welcome." Meg strode past her into the ladies' room on the other side of the room. Anna glanced at Dani, feeling humiliated. Too shocked to talk, she turned around and left, holding back unexpected tears.

Chapter 19

He who walks with the wise will be wise. Proverbs 13:20

Josh arrived at the hospital a while later. As he stepped into the waiting room Dani spotted him.

"Hi Josh! Is Eric with you?" Coffee in hand, Dani smiled and gave him a careful hug. She led the way to Meg.

"Josh, this is Glen's wife, Meg. Meg, this is my friend Josh Marineta."

"No, I'm alone today. How are you, Dani? Good to see you." He redirected his gaze to Meg Stuart.

"Hi Meg, I'm so sorry about Glen," offering his hand. Meg squeezed it briefly and let it go.

"Nice to meet you Josh. Glen's going to make it. They tell me he arrived in time. How did you know about Glen?" she asked giving Dani a puzzled look and then turned back to Josh with a jolt. "Marineta! You're the one trying to meet with the council!"

"I happened to be in Marin last night because I had a meeting scheduled with Anna. Then the fire broke out. So, I did what I could to help. Eric Miller, our Fire Chief in Bellalto, was with me. He acted quickly and brought in his team as extra help. We were with Glen when he collapsed. I'm on my way home and wanted to know how he is today."

"Well, thank you for coming." Meg said grudgingly. "It was his heart, Josh. I never knew he had a problem! The doctor said it was stress related. Anna's nothing but trouble." Her face flushed and eyes flashed.

"Why do you say that? She was upset about Glen. She's coming today to see how he is and if she can do anything."

"I know! She already came. I sent her packing! She's the reason he's in the hospital."

Found By the Water

Meg stopped talking as she became aware of Dani's hand resting gently on her arm. She impatiently shook off her friend. "Dani? What?"

"Perhaps now is not the time to get into all this. Why don't you check on Glen?" Dani walked with her in the direction of Glen's CICU bay. Looking back at Josh, Dani smiled apologetically on behalf of her friend. "See you later. It's so nice of you to stop by and to help Marin like you did. I'll talk to you later."

"I hope Glen improves quickly." Josh walked toward the cafeteria.

❧

He saw Anna sitting alone at a back table. Her shoulders hunched slightly in a self-protective manner; unconsciously trying not to draw attention to herself. He walked over with his cup. "May I join you?" Anna looked up. Her face said no, but she nodded.

Sitting down, he said, "I went up to check on Glen. I ran into Meg Stuart and Dani Evans. Do you know Dani?"

"I do not know Meg or Dani very well but I know who they are. I went up there too. Meg was rude. Frankly, I'm in shock that she was so hateful toward me."

"I'm sorry Anna. She's upset right now. She was less than cordial to me too."

"The fact is," Anna continued lost in her own thoughts, "I had no idea there was so much anger toward me in Marin. The fire seems to have brought out the worst in a lot of people. You saw how angry they were at my house last night. I had no idea how much they dislike me." Anna said quietly. "And I'm upset for never asking for emergency phone numbers and for not making an effort to get to know them personally."

"You can change that Anna," Josh offered the idea, "if you want. Together we can address the key component of the economic decline in Marin, water. If you would let go of your anger long enough to explore the possibilities available, your community would be most grateful judging by what I witnessed last night."

She raised her hands, palms up, with a slight shrug, "I don't know where to begin. I've never been outright mean though, like Meg was to me." She stopped suddenly, looking at him sheepishly. "Well, not to most people. I owe you an apology. I haven't been inclined to like you much. I'm beginning to realize you're different. I'm trying to figure it out. Part of me doesn't believe you."

Found By the Water

"In many ways, I understand why you don't think much of my family. Dad and I are trying to change things for the better. We have no intention of taking advantage. In fact, we are working toward the opposite. We want to permanently improve valley economy and mountain relationships. All this bitterness has gone on long enough."

"Well, it seems like I have some fences to mend. But first, I think I need to hear what you have to say. Are you still willing?" Then, she saw Dani Evans walking toward them. "Dani's here. I'd better get going and let you get on with your day." She started to stand up.

"Please stay. You'll like Dani. She's genuinely a nice person. Please sit down and get to know her. Hi Dani, look who I ran into. Anna, this is my friend Dani Evans. You probably know each other, though."

"Hi Anna. I'm glad we had the chance to meet again this morning. I'd like to apologize for how Meg greeted you a few minutes ago. I hope you get to meet her at a better time." Dani greeted her warmly.

"Nice to meet you formally, Dani. Well, I'd better get home. There's a mess waiting for me on Main Street and I'm meeting with the Bolton's later. Maybe I'll see you again some time." Anna stood up and headed toward the exit.

"I'd like that, Anna." Dani said with a smile.

Dani and Josh sat in comfortable silence for a few minutes. Dani spoke first. "I don't understand the animosity that Meg has toward Anna, Josh. I didn't grow up in Marin. I suppose it's something from their younger years. But I believe the Lord is working something in all this; more than the water plan Eric mentioned to me."

"I've been feeling a bit like a failure because of my inability to connect with Anna. I thought she was my best shot at uniting the valley with the Water Authority. I'm wondering if I should try to work with another town first."

"Josh my friend, it'll take more than your wonderful personality to achieve your purpose with the situation.

We need to trust that God is moving in bigger ways than you and I can see." Dani smiled. She kissed his cheek and stood up to go back to Meg. Josh stood with her. He had a lot to think about on the way home.

Chapter 20

Be angry and do not sin. Ephesians 4:26

Around 4:00 pm, Dani asked, "Do you feel comfortable going home tonight Meg?"

"I made reservations at a B&B around the corner. I'll ride back to Marin with you, pack a few things and drive back. I want to stay nearby for a few days until Glen is in a regular room. Are you ready to go back now?"

"Sure. I'll get the car." Dani was ready to go too; they both needed sleep. Ten minutes later they were on their way.

"Meg, would you like to talk about how you're feeling about all this? It helps sometimes."

"I'm still a little numb; mixed with fear and anger." Meg pushed her hair off her face and exhaled.

"I understand the fear. But I don't understand your anger at Anna. How is Glen's heart attack her fault?"

Meg did not reply.

"Something had to have triggered it. It's fierce and not like you. It doesn't make sense. I saw the shock on Anna's face. She didn't understand."

"You didn't grow up here. This town has always been about the Marin family. Anna acts superior to the rest of us mere mortals. She never did much after school except work in her gardens and her comfortable town jobs."

"Is that all you have? What does that have to do with Glen? I've known you a long time and you're better than this." Dani gently replied.

"No, that's not all. You know she runs the town. She wants her own way, thinks it's the best way and doesn't like to listen to opposing views. Glen comes home so stressed because of her unreasonableness."

Found By the Water

She turned her head away from Dani holding back tears and thinking *'Why is she attacking me? I'm the injured party. Rather, Glen is. Still, I don't deserve this.'*

"Why hasn't anyone talked to her privately to explain how the council feels about her methods? Who are her friends? Could they help her understand?"

"I barely know her and I don't know who her friends are. She doesn't socialize much. But she hasn't made the best decisions when it comes to men. She's living with a guy now. Come to think of it, I haven't seen Matt around in a while." Listening to herself, she sounded petty and peevish. "Dani, I don't want to talk about her anymore. I have enough on my mind."

"Because I love you, friend, I need to say your anger isn't going to help Glen recover quickly." Dani spoke truth. "Would you pray about it? It's not good for you either. Whenever I think how Jesus taught us to forgive like he did for you and me, it sobers me enough to work it all out with him. He has forgiven me everything I've done wrong; you, too." She pulled into Meg's driveway.

"This isn't the time for a bible study. Leave it be." Meg quickly opened the car door and swung her legs out. "Thank you for being with me at the hospital. You're a good friend. I needed you. I hope I'll be as good as you are someday. I promise I'll think about this some more." She walked to her front door, turning around to give a quick wave.

Driving back to the hospital a half-hour later, Meg tried to push the conversation to the back of her mind but it would not stay there. Feeling discomfited about her animosity toward Anna, she thought, *'Dani made a lot of sense; the childhood stuff has no relevance today. Yet my anger is real but nothing readily comes to mind as the source of it, except me being mean-spirited.'*

"Lord Jesus, I love you. I have such peace when you forgive me. Why can't I forgive?" She asked him, speaking as if he were right there in the car next to her. "I don't understand the source of the anger. Show me."

Pulling into a parking space, she sensed an inner nudge she knew was from the Holy Spirit. *'You are looking at her outward appearance and think it's her heart. I see and know her for who she really is.'*[5]

Found By the Water

"Don't her outward actions reflect her heart, Lord? Wasn't I taught that we are what we think?"[6] She continued to speak aloud. An immediate response was not forthcoming.

Meg turned her thoughts to the man she loved and walked toward the hospital entrance. *'I'll ask Dani. She'll know how to explain it to me.'*

Chapter 21

Bread gained by deceit is sweet to man. Proverbs 20:17

That same day, the day after the fire, Brea realized she had not heard from Sean since his parent's party a couple of weeks ago. She had lingered at her desk a few times. *'Is he avoiding me?'* she wondered to herself. Her interview at the Farin' had gone well once she shared her idea with the editor for increasing readership. It had been easier than she thought it would be. He was more concerned with expanding subscriptions than being scrupulous. She was hired the same day.

She knew from the letters already coming in that the people were fed up with the economic state of the town. She was not sure yet what Josh wanted to discuss with the Mayor or if Anna would be willing. In the meantime, she had a plan for stirring up even more doubt about Anna. It could be successful and they would ask for Anna's resignation. *'Then it'll be my chance to run the town. I can't wait to tell Sean.'* The phone rang in her hand.

"Hello." Brea feigned disinterest.

"Brea, this is Sean. Are you free for dinner tonight? I heard Josh Marineta was in town recently. Do you know why?"

"I can meet for dinner. Where do you want to go?" She replied.

"Meet me in Bellalto at the Rapids on Main, like last time. At 7:00 pm." Sean stated.

"Sure thing. B-" Sean abruptly ended the call.

Shrugging, she pocketed her phone and mentally went over the things she wanted to tell him. Instead, her thoughts turned to the perpetual sadness that weighed her down. Growing up in a big family, she had gotten lost in the demands on her parents to provide for and raise so many children. Being one of ten had been a challenge for Brea. She learned to form devious schemes that would put her in favor with her parents.

Found By the Water

She became so good at it she did not recognize that there were other more rewarding ways to achieve her goals and obtain what she needed or wanted; ways that would foster relationships. Now she was doing it again and it was exhausting. *'Maybe someday when I have all that I want and deserve, I'll be able to just live without all this effort,'* she thought and pushed aside her emotions.

Brea glanced at the time. It was 10:00 am. She had a rafting party to meet in Bellalto. She grabbed her go bag and headed out the door.

When she arrived at the put-in or starting ramp, her river party was moving purposefully around. Most were experienced and had rafted with her before. They were helping the less experienced to gear up and rig their crafts. She could hear them relaying safety reminders as they did. The Ranger was there checking the fit and condition of life jackets, a requirement the Pettrie's insisted on.

Brea rapidly gauged the group's ability to navigate the run she had mapped out for them. Since the ratio of experienced versus inexperienced rafters was high, she knew the Class 3 rapids would be challenging but not deadly. They would create some excitement for newer rafters and still challenge the others. She stepped up and began to review the final safety instructions. Then she assigned the most capable people to be in-charge of each craft. Brea, as the trip and river rescue leader, gathered the major rescue gear. Once on the water, she insisted that the less experienced join in some river safety exercises with simulated events. Then they were ready to launch.

The first part of the trip was exhilarating. By the time they arrived at the portage take-out around the dam, they were tired but happy. They took their time navigating the 30-degree decline of the portage route and soon reached the lower river. They put-in again three miles above Marin and made good time moving downriver by staying where the currents were strongest. They relaxed a little while manning the craft.

At the trip's take-out, two Pettrie vehicles were waiting to haul equipment, gear, and people back to the starting ramp. It had been a good run and Brea was ready to enjoy dinner with Sean. After saying her good-byes to the rafters, she drove to headquarters to get ready for the evening and walked into Rapids on Main right on time. Sean stood from his place at the bar as she walked in and they were seated quickly.

Found By the Water

"Your hair is wet, Brea. Did you have a trip today?" He looked around and visibly relaxed when he saw no one had noticed. He held out her chair.

"I did. Loved every minute of it!" She smiled still in the adrenaline high. "This group was-"

"So," Sean interrupted. "Have you learned yet why Josh was in Marin?"

Brea was silent for a moment. Determinedly, she finished her statement. "As I was saying, this group was the finest I've led. This is a great job."

"Well, that's good to hear. You're becoming one of our most experienced trip leaders. Glad to hear you're happy." His mind was on meeting his father's demands for information.

"What have you learned?" He asked again.

"I only know he's been trying to meet with the Mayor. Anna doesn't know but she thinks he might want to raise water rates. The Council voted to meet with Josh to hear him out. Did you know there was a fire in town yesterday? A diner on Main. The Fire Chief collapsed. I heard that the lower river seemed higher than normal. I noticed it myself after the portage. It was high water downstream from the dam. It's well above the normal levels." Brea stopped to sip her drink. She watched Sean as he absorbed this information.

"Dad doesn't seem to know about high water. At least he didn't say anything to me. I wonder why and how that happened. The headgates are always set precisely. That's good information, Brea. Anything else?"

She smiled at the compliment. "I've been hired at the Marin Farin' newspaper as a part-time editor of the op-ed page. I have access to letters from a lot of people who are fed up with the economic decline in town. Anna doesn't have their confidence anymore. They think she could have done more by now to improve the situation. I have an idea that could increase their level of animosity toward her."

"What's your idea?" Sean was clearly interested.

"I'd rather not say more now. Let's leave it there, Sean."

Chapter 22

The end of a thing is better than the beginning. Ecclesiastes 7:8

Rob held up letters. "I've heard from some of the board," he said a few days later. Josh and Eric were relaxing on the front porch with him. "Three are related to resignations from the board. A few affirm support. Losing three board members is not as bad as it could have been. Frankly, I didn't know what to expect. While I'm sorry to lose knowledgeable people, this opens the opportunity to bring in Valley representatives."

"Who resigned from the company?" Josh asked.

"Tom Pettrie is leaving the Water Authority entirely. Two others who are close to him are resigning from the Board but opted to stay with the Authority for now. Tom has a following, it seems. He said the time is right for him. His public explanation is that he's turning over his business to his son and wants the time to support the transition properly. Privately he told me he doesn't agree with the direction we're going. The others gave some mild version of Tom's reasons."

"I've always wondered why Tom chose to continue working after inheriting the Pettrie fortune. What do you think about those who are leaving the board but not the Authority?" Eric asked. "Do you think they will support the changes?"

"I know them. They'll support the changes once they understand them better. I think they're taking a wait and see attitude. They don't want to make drastic life decisions at this point."

"Dad, we can work with this. I haven't yet had a chance to talk to Anna formally but something is happening in her. The fire helped her see that changes are needed. People in Marin are putting pressure on her. Eric made a big impression, working with their fire crew and improving river levels the way he did. He even went over to her house after they contained the fire to introduce himself and talk with her."

Found By the Water

"She let me pray while I was there. This whole thing shook her up." Eric said.

"She thought you would charge for the extra water. That it was a ploy to take advantage of a bad situation. She couldn't comprehend at first that it was a gift. She wants to meet you Dad. Who would have thought it would take something this devastating to open her eyes?"

"I have an idea who from Marin you could ask to join the Board. Glen Stuart." Eric held his hands up, palms out. "I know, I know. It's not the right timing but when he recovers, it will be."

Pacing now, energy flowed from Eric. "In the meantime, I'm going to see when he can have visitors and ask if he'd be interested in a joint effort to improve our fire procedures. Since I'm doing the same thing in Bellalto we could pool our knowledge. I was watching him the other day and he knows what he's doing. He's been up against some tough breaks which we've started to fix with more water. There are serious equipment needs too. I can help with some improvements in department budget planning and he can help me with the people side of things. His men respect him. He's a great mentor and I know I need one. He's been Chief a lot longer than I have."

"That's a great idea! Why stop with Marin?" Rob replied. "I see the potential for a regional effort to develop a team of experts."

"Josh, when are you going to meet with Anna next?" Rob asked.

"It's going to be soon. I'm confirming the date with her tomorrow."

"Invite her for dinner when you talk to her. It's time to show her the journal. But right now, we'd better leave for the board meeting." Rob and Josh headed that way and Eric left with his head full of strategies.

Walking home after the meeting, Rob broke the silence and smiled at his son. "It's a good beginning. We all parted friends even though we don't agree. Good progress has been made during the past month."

"I agree but I'm still not sure where I am with Anna. I have yet to make a real connection. And something seems to be going on with Tom. He was distracted. After all his attitude during the last meeting, I expected more from him tonight. Have you learned anything about the report discrepancies we've noticed?"

"Good instinct with Tom; all is not in the open. I'm still gathering information through the resources I've engaged. As soon as I know more, I'll tell you. You were on the right track; though. Funds are missing.

Found By the Water

We're learning patience as we move out in faith. Trials exercise our trust in God.[7] He knows how to lead us even when we don't understand the route. And God is allowing Anna, and some other people, to catch up. The delay is about giving her time to turn to Jesus, rather than rushing to make a successful project. His heart is always for people first. He's the only one who knows what's necessary to change us."

"I get it. The way you explain it, I'm right on target." Silence resumed the rest of the way home as both turned their thoughts to the One who had set them on this course.

Chapter 23

The integrity of the upright will guide them. Proverbs 11:3

Four days after the fire, Anna walked down Main Street to survey the damage and progress. Crews were still clearing the rubble. The fire had cooled enough for the insurance adjustors and fire investigators to assess the damage. Anna knew by looking at it that it was going to be bad for the Bolton's. Wondering if they would ever recover, she turned toward her office, thinking again about how she could help them. The first meeting with them had been difficult. Gus had looked devastated as Jennie cried. The diner was their livelihood. *'I've never had to worry about lack. Has it made me immune to other people's pain?'* she thought.

She picked up the prior week's copy of the Marin Farin'. It was more gossip than news but it was one way she learned what was going on. In her office, she flipped through it while enjoying a cup of coffee. A photo about halfway down the front page caught her eye. Someone had captured her leaning into Glen at the fire scene, pointing toward the diner immediately before the last wall fell. A short article accompanied.

What Don't We Know?

The hottest fire in Marin for a decade is cooling. Our Fire Chief is still in the hospital. It was a miracle that others were not impacted, considering the chronic public water deficiency and high rates. Our Mayor and Council Chair is acting like nothing happened. What could she be saying to Chief Stuart? Could there be a cover up?

There was no byline, no claim to the inflammatory words. Talking to Glen would have to wait. She decided to keep working on the Bolton solution for now. The paper was two days old and no one had said anything yet. She began to draw up a plan that might work for the Bolton's recovery but found concentration elusive. Second thoughts about the article crept back. She reached for the phone to call the Farin' editor. As she did, she looked up to see Dani standing in the doorway.

Found By the Water

"Hi Anna. I came to file a building permit for a new construction site. I'm on my way to lunch. Would you like to join me?" Dani smiled.

Anna paused. A flicker of some undefinable emotion flitted across her face. "I don't have a lot of time today but why not? It'll be nice. Where are you thinking of going?" Anna motioned for Dani to come in.

"I was heading to the Wild River Café. I haven't been there yet. Have you?" Dani stepped into the office and sat on the sofa Anna used for informal meetings.

"No. I haven't. I've been distracted recently." She straightened papers on her desk, locked a drawer and stood up. "Okay. I'm ready."

Dani pulled into traffic and headed out of town. "Wild River opened about a month ago. It's been long enough to work out all the kinks. I've heard it's an interesting place. Even the locals are enjoying it. Especially now that the diner is gone."

"Gone for now. I hope once the investigators and insurance adjustors finish, the results will allow the Bolton's to rebuild, if they want. How far is the Wild River from Marin?"

"Twenty minutes tops, on the main road away from Bellalto."

"That's close enough for people to get used to the distance. The Bolton's created a special place serving an immediate local population of businesses and the surrounding residential area. It would be a great loss if they decide not to rebuild."

"Anna. I'm going to cost the job and give them as reasonable a bid as I can. Do you think they'd be interested? I don't know if they've seen what my crew can do."

Anna hid her surprise well. "It wouldn't hurt to ask them. I've been trying to think of ways I could help them. And the town, too."

The ride was relaxing. The Wild River Café, as a terminus for rafting tours launched farther upriver near Bellalto, had already become a favorite spot for guides and rafters. Dani and Anna road in silence for a while, listening to music.

"This music is different. What kind is it?" Anna asked after she had started listening to the words.

"It's worship music."

"You mean, like singing about God? It's a lot different than I've heard the few times I've been in a church."

"It's more singing *to* God, than about him, in this case."

Found By the Water

"What do you like about it?" Anna asked with real interest. "Why do you sing to God?"

"It's one way of acknowledging what he's done for me. It reminds me of his attributes and promises. I respond to his love and presence. My mind turns from all the things I can't control to his abilities. I'm encouraged by the words."

"God is all that for you?"

"He is and more. Worship is different than just singing or entertainment. It's an act of adoration; a way of honoring him." Dani smiled at Anna. "It brings me to a place where I can hear him."

Anna didn't know what to say. She didn't understand so she smiled. "God and I, well, we aren't well acquainted. It seems important to you and I'm happy for that. The music is nice." She was relieved when she saw their destination come into view.

The Wild River Café was on the Bella Chute River. The unassuming exterior blended into the surrounding area. The water was calm and docks were available. There was a separate dining area for rafters where they could celebrate a successful run in their gear without tempering end-of-run exuberance. Diners from the main room were visiting with them. Anna was comfortable at once when they walked in and sat at the last available table by a window facing the river. The menu included a large selection of healthy choices, with catchy names related to popular area vacation activities.

Preparing to relax and enjoy the experience, Anna saw someone start toward them with a wave. Excusing herself, Dani stood up to greet her friend. As they talked, Anna looked the menu over and made her choice.

"How nice to see you again," the friend said with a hug. "I've been thinking about the bible study discussion the other night. Meg seemed preoccupied. Have you seen her since?"

"Hi Kate," Dani quietly interrupted, "I'd like you to meet Anna Marin. We're getting to know each other over lunch. Let's plan for coffee another time." Their lunch choices arrived as she finished greeting Kate.

"Hi Anna. Nice to meet you." Kate walked back to her table.

They were quiet, taking their first bites. Suddenly, Anna looked at Dani. "Meg Stuart considers herself a Christian?" Her face registered disbelief. "I've always thought the God thing never really changed anyone for long. Meg confirms it. I've never thought God cared about me."

Found By the Water

"I know he does. I was surprised because I've never seen Meg treat anyone quite that way. I saw how hurt you were and I'm sorry that happened."

"That's kind of you to say but it doesn't excuse Meg."

"I know you both grew up in Marin. Did something happen in the past that could have caused her reaction?"

"Not that I'm aware. I barely know her. I didn't hang around with anyone growing up; still don't. Being a Marin, in a town named Marin, hasn't been easy." Glancing at her phone, she took a final sip of water and pushed her chair away from the table. "If you are ready, I should get back. I have a lot to do today."

The return ride to Marin was quiet. Anna pushed Meg to the back of her mind as she considered more ideas to help the Bolton's, as well as Marin.

"Anna, I asked you to lunch because I want to get to know you. I'm glad I did. I hope we can do this again."

"I'd like that. Thank you for your invitation today and for thinking about the diner solution, too. Let's plan to discuss our ideas in more depth soon." Anna stepped out of the car, her mind already back on her recovery plan.

As she turned to walk up the steps to her office, she saw Brea leaving the Farin' office, although it was far enough away that she couldn't be sure. Walking by Glen's empty office she paused, feeling unexpectedly forlorn. She realized she had never told him how much she appreciated his ability to bring people together to solve a problem and wondered if she could learn from him. Then she remembered the two words he had spoken to her right after he collapsed the night of the fire, to keep her eyes on Brea.

Chapter 24

Learn to do good. Isaiah 1:17

The Farin' article had spurred Anna's determination to meet with Josh and hear what he had to say. She knew that something had to be done about the water situation. And she could be as wrong about him as Meg was about her.

"Josh, this is Anna. How are you today?" She began.

"Hi Anna. I'm fine. I hope you are calling to re-schedule our meeting with the council. I'm free tomorrow evening if the council can meet."

"That happens to be the time of our scheduled meeting; 7:00 pm sharp. Let's plan on it. Can you be in my office at 6:30 pm? I'll give you a quick run through of the order of business."

"Sure thing. Game time! See you then." Josh smiled to himself.

He arrived the next evening and presented himself at Anna's office door. She invited him to sit on the sofa, offered him water with a smile and handed him a copy of the meeting agenda where he was listed first.

"I'd like to introduce you. I'm sorry to say that I may have presented you in an unfavorable light in the past, although some of them urged me to get to know you before making judgments. They gave me good advice." Anna hesitated. "I must say that I'm beginning to think I was completely wrong in my initial assessment of you. I'm willing to hear your plan. We'll want a chance to ask questions. It's not often we get to say our piece to a Marineta. Are you ready for anything?"

"Yes. I'm ready. It's important that we all understand each other. I want to hear everything they have to say to me. Thanks, Anna, for this opportunity."

Found By the Water

"Okay, then. Let's roll. Everyone should be here by now." As she led him to the conference room, all heads turned silently toward them. They looked at Anna first as usual, then turned to Josh, the real person of interest. A Marineta was finally in their midst. Anna approached the table, took her seat and the others joined her. Josh was the last to sit as his way of honoring the group. Anna confirmed that Glen was ready for the conference call from his hospital room. After a few encouraging words to him, Anna brought the meeting to order.

"This is a special meeting tonight. For the first time in Marin history a member of the Marineta family has asked to meet with us. I'd like to introduce you to Joshua Marineta. He is the son of the current Marineta patriarch, Robert. As you know, his grandfather, Mike, passed recently and Rob has come to the helm of the Chute Valley Water Authority."

Anna paused to take a sip of water. "I'm sorry for your loss, Josh" she said to him.

"Josh has informed me that he and his father intend to make some changes to CVWA's policies with valley towns. To be honest, as you know, I didn't trust him at first. Then we all saw how Josh and Eric stepped in to fight alongside us the night of the fire. Rob, whom I have not met yet, quietly authorized increasing the river volume a couple of days before the fire started. Eric Miller, Bellalto's Fire Chief, requested it again during the fire at Josh's prompting. You all must have noticed by now that the river is higher than normal for the first time in our lifetime and without charge to the valley. I'm grateful for their assistance. Without their kindness, we may have lost Main Street."

During this introduction, eyes around the table kept shifting between Anna and Josh. Some nodded to him in silent thanks. He noticed that one woman kept her eyes on Anna and only stole quick looks at him every now and then. There was a wariness in her expression. She had introduced herself as Brea.

"I have not yet heard all Josh's ideas. I thought it would be best to hear it for the first time with the entire Council present. Then we can ask our questions and decide how to proceed. Does anyone disagree?" Anna looked around the room. Everyone agreed, including Brea grudgingly.

"All right then. Let's proceed. Josh, tell us what you are planning."

"It's great to finally meet you. My Dad and I would like to see an improvement in the relationship between the mountain and valley, on a

Found By the Water

business and personal level. We have long been unhappy with the ill will between us and are well-aware that the division started long ago within the Marineta family. We want to end it and aim to start now with your help. Marin is the first town we're engaging with because from our research it's the hardest hit. We're saddened by the depth of the animosity that characterizes our business relationships."

"May I interrupt for a moment?" Jacob asked.

"Sure." Josh turned to him.

"What do you mean that the division started within the Marineta family way back when?"

"I've gone back into family archives to learn that the two brothers who founded the area did not agree on how to use the abundant water supply we have been blessed with. The older and more forceful man wanted to control the water for his own advantage and his brother didn't agree. It caused a permanent rift in the family. It is our belief that the familial division is the origin of the ill will between the valley and mountain areas. We are persuaded that it also perpetuated the nature of business practices and personal relationships." Josh paused for a moment to gauge reactions.

There was silence as the council members absorbed this new information. Josh had implied his relatives had brought years of hardship to the valley. He had also honored them by recognizing that Marin had suffered the most and wanted to start improvements with them. Only Brea's face indicated any negative emotion, her eyes narrowing from time to time. Jacob sat up straighter and looked at Josh with interest.

The oldest Council member was the only one with a ready word. "I've never heard that story before. Have you Anna?" Anna shook her head without speaking. "Maybe we need to hear the rest of what you have to say, Josh."

"My Dad and I want to end this by understanding why Marin never sends representatives to CVWA's annual public forums. Why don't you send in annual usage reports so we have realistic data for decisions and why agree to such disadvantageous contracts with the Authority?"

"Would it make any difference?" Anna asked. "It never has."

"I know my grandfather, and his before him, were not easy to approach but when presented with logical well-substantiated facts, my grandfather would listen. Granted it took some doing. It seems you are not the only town that gave up. On the other hand, after asking similar questions to the

Authority's decision makers, we learned they also stopped trying. We want to change this practice."

"How do you propose to do that?" Sally asked.

"There are a couple initial steps we can take. The first one is that you agree to prepare and present the requested reports to CVWA well in advance of the rate change analysis every year. Make sure that Marin's usage requirements are accurate. We'll have an annual review meeting with you to ensure we fully understand your needs before beginning the rate process. The second thing is that we are asking for a Marin representative to join the CVWA Board to engage in business decisions that impact the valley and mountain regions alike." He had everyone's attention.

"There are three things you need to decide. Since we have already notified you that the reports are due one month from today, would you agree to provide them this year? We've scheduled our annual usage review meeting six weeks from today. Would you join us to help understand our mutual needs? Lastly, it is our hope that you will decide who is the best person to be Marin's Board representative. We would like them to attend the next Board meeting scheduled in eight weeks. That's the extent of our plan at this point. These three changes to our business relationship will begin to repair our historically unhappy association. Are you willing?" Josh sat back and waited, having done his best. Now he would trust the Lord to work it out.

"Are there any other questions or comments for Josh?" Anna's question met with silence. She let it continue for a minute. "Would you like to discuss among ourselves before answering him?"

"I think we should have the discussion with him in the room." Jacob replied. "Everything he said makes sense. All this bad emotion has clouded both sides. I'm all for moving ahead with these three simple steps. We already prepare the reports. But all we use them for is to gripe."

"I agree with Jacob." Glen said over the phone. "It's a bigger step for CVWA than it is for Marin. If they are willing, we should be. The stress of the bad relationship almost killed me! We need more water, period. It makes sense that we ask for what we need. Josh has agreed to a better rate determination process. It would be foolish not to accept the offered handshake."

Found By the Water

Brea crossed her arms over her chest. "How do you know we can trust them? They may draw us in and then show their true Marineta colors. We don't know Rob and he's the important one. Josh has no real authority. From what I hear, the Chair never delegates his authority."

"How do we know if we can trust anyone? We give them a chance to earn it. I'm willing. The water situation can't get any worse." Sally replied.

The discussion continued for several minutes and then Anna spoke. "It's time to vote. First, I have to say that I've been persuaded after listening to Josh, to meet his three requests. What harm can it do? I agree with you. How much worse can it get? We all saw firsthand how bad it was during the fire. They acted honorably through it all. That is enough for me to proceed. What have you decided?" They expelled a collective breath.

"All in favor, raise your right hand. Glen, say Aye." Six hands went up, with an 'Aye' from Glen. They all looked at Brea, who was scowling back at them.

"All opposed, raise your right hand." Defiantly, only Brea's hand went into the air.

"Josh, we have decided to meet your requests and deadlines." Anna said with a smile. "I have one more question for the Council. Do you want to nominate our CVWA Board representative now? We can do it by closed ballot. Yes?" Anna began handing out makeshift ballots and gave them a few minutes to write. Glen texted his nomination to Anna. Once all nominations were back, Anna opened them and laid them out in front of her. There was one nomination for Dani Evans, one for Gus Bolton, five for Glen Stuart. One person had abstained from voting. Choosing to ignore it for now, Anna reported the results. "Glen, we nominated you to be our Board representative. Do you want to think about it before making a decision to accept or decline?"

Glen was silent while he took time to pray, as he considered the responsibility and impact on his role as Fire Chief. He knew the correct decision in an instant.

"I accept." He said aloud. "Who better than I to discuss the risks of not working out a viable contract with CVWA? Of course, I need to talk to Meg, but knowing that I'll have the opportunity to improve the fire risk factor is a huge relief. I am honored to be trusted with this responsibility."

Found By the Water

"Thank you, Glen, for accepting. You have our complete trust. Now, we have other agenda items to discuss before we adjourn the meeting. Thank you for coming today Josh. I'll be in touch with you soon. We're looking forward to working this out with CVWA." Anna stood with him, walked him to the door and shook his hand. When she turned back to take her seat at the table, she received an ugly look from Brea.

They addressed the rest of the agenda items quickly. Immediately after the meeting adjourned, Anna leaned over to Brea and said quietly. "I've learned something unpleasant and would like to discuss it with you now."

Brea bristled and scowled. She stayed seated while Anna said good-bye to the others. "I talked to the Farin' editor who told me you had given him the fire photo and planted suspicion in his mind. Why did you do that?"

Brea stiffened and stuck out her chin slightly. "Something wasn't right about that whole scenario. How do we know you aren't covering up something?"

"Because we aren't. It's as simple as that. We've reviewed the inspection evaluation reports which found nothing out of the ordinary. Why would you do this?"

"What did you really see and point out to Glen? I don't like how you've been acting lately. I looked up to you, as the no nonsense in-charge Council Chair you've always been. Like I want to be when I-." cutting off abruptly.

"Never mind. It's not important." She glanced at her watch. "I'm out of time. I need to leave now. I hope you think about what I said." She got up and walked toward the door.

"Brea!" Anna followed her. "Why did you abstain from the last vote tonight? It was you, wasn't it?"

"Because I would have been the better choice, Anna. Now I really do have to leave."

Chapter 25

Judge not. Matthew 7:1

Glen had improved quickly. Now in a regular room, he felt well enough to go home. "Meg darlin'. You're exhausted. I love that you've been by my side but it's time you went home. I'll be there with you soon."

Meg was having trouble keeping her eyes open. Deep sleep had eluded her ever since Glen's heart attack. "Good idea, but I hate to leave you. I'll call you to say goodnight. Perhaps you'll be discharged earlier than we think."

"I know I have to find a way to manage the stress in my life. I feel like it's been an uphill battle for a long time now. I hope God sends me a solution before I go back to work."

They kissed goodbye and Meg left. Glen picked up the copy of the latest Farin' issue to flip through until he fell asleep again. His eyes went immediately to the photo on the front page. He read the insinuating article quickly and felt his blood pressure rising. In typical resolution mode, he made a few phone calls to the inspection and insurance teams, asking them to email him their reports and to review them with him for any unusual findings.

Unaware that Glen was working from his hospital bed, Meg's drive home was uneventful except for the internal unrest she felt. Her mind went to the morning after Glen's collapse. She had not known whether he would live. Then her reaction to Anna's visit came flooding back into memory. She felt a sense of deep remorse and embarrassment.

"Lord," she prayed. "Dani was right. Why don't I like Anna? What was it you reminded me of that night? I don't know her. I have to talk to Dani about that."

Found By the Water

"Call Dani," she spoke into the phone. "Hi. I'm on my way home. The doctor is discharging Glen this week. Yes, that's good news. Would you meet me at my house later? There's something I want to discuss with you. Okay, see you soon."

By the time Dani arrived, Meg had been able to sleep for several hours. They went out to the patio to watch the sunset. "Dani, I need to apologize that you witnessed my ugly behavior to Anna. I don't like her, yet I don't know why. After you encouraged me a couple of weeks ago to think about it, the Lord clearly showed me he looks at people's hearts, not at outward appearances. Would you explain the verse that says, 'As a man thinks in his heart, so he is'? I take people at face value. I've always believed people's actions reflect their heart."

"When I read the verses before that one in Proverbs 23:7, they show that outward actions can be deceiving." Dani explained. "It is not helpful to make decisions about a person's character or true thoughts and feelings by how they act publicly. I've known people who seemed confident until I knew them better. Once they trusted me, they revealed more of their insecurities. In fact, before we became friends, I thought you were shallow. You loved to talk about vacations taken and the next one you were planning. I've since learned that you are caring and usually, kind. You are well informed about the subjects that interest you. There is depth to you I couldn't see at first."

Meg was silent for a minute. "Growing up we didn't have a lot. We had what we needed and not enough for extras like vacations. My parents did their best. But I had always dreamed about visiting the coast, the Sequoias, and the Grand Canyon. I'd listen to other kids talk about their travels and I'd tell myself that one day I'd be able to talk about my experiences. I may go too far sometimes. I don't like being thought of as shallow.

"I understand what you're saying though, Dani. Anna wasn't unfriendly with anyone growing up. She just didn't go out of her way to spend time with us. It was always about the gardens and jobs. She lived in a nice house. We'd see the family leave for vacations. I thought she was snobby. Since no one really knew her, others thought the same thing. She's still like that."

"Did I tell you that Anna and I recently had lunch at the Wild River Café? She seems a person who is comfortable with her own company and yet, a bit lonely. But I did not see any sign that she is snobby. There is a bit of aloofness. Some people do that out of self-protection. They stand back a little from people to get their bearings before engaging."

"I've never thought about that before. It sounds like you think her standoffishness is due to social awkwardness or some other reason."

"I do. It's an example of how people sometimes present a different public face than they would to those who love them. It's the trust factor. They don't know how to engage with others. She may have tried making overtures and it didn't go well. She acts like she doesn't care; and may believe it by now. As hard as she tries to hide it, I saw something caring and genuine about her. You know, she's worried about the Bolton's. She worried about Glen. And she thinks God doesn't care about her. It saddens me."

"I'm beginning to understand I've been unfair. I may have been quick to falsely judge her."

"I will tell you this," Dani replied. "When we ran into Kate at the Café, she mentioned bible study and you in the same breath. Anna was surprised to learn you were a believer and was put off by that. You hurt her. She did not understand why you were angry."

Shame and sadness flowed through Meg. She prided herself in being a good judge of character. *'A judge is what I've been.'* she thought.

Aloud she said, "I need to apologize to Anna. But first I have some heart issues of my own to take care of."

❦

Meg stood at her kitchen window with cup in hand the next morning, staring into the early morning mist. Her thoughts wandered over the events since the fire. Glen was recovering well. Now she had to face an uncomfortable truth about herself. She had judged Anna unfairly for years without getting to know her. The realization of this simple fact had affected her relationship with Christ and hindered others to know his love. She had to fix this, or at least do whatever she could to rectify the situation. Meg knew what she needed to do and it was not going to be easy. Sighing, she dumped her bitter drink down the drain. Straightening her shoulders, she started to get ready for the day.

"Father forgive me. Give me courage to do the right thing now. Let Anna see your goodness despite my behavior. While we're talking Lord, I didn't realize I had made vacations and travel such a focal point in my life. You've been good to me in that regard. I need to be more aware of other's feelings. I may have inadvertently made others feel like I did as a child. I give that part of myself to you to change. Teach me." Meg prayed.

Chapter 26

Be kind to one another, forgiving. Ephesians 4:32

For Anna, the same hot and humid day began in her extended gardens located on family land where the Bolton's might want to rebuild. She worked steadily for several hours to reap the remains of the harvest thinking about her own future. *'Why am I still blindly following in my family's expectations when my real love is horticulture? I've longed for years to grow on a larger scale.'*

She sat back on her heels as the realization dawned on her. She saw an opportunity to use her knowledge and love of farming by establishing a true farm to table operation on another plot of land. Gus and Jennie might make a faster financial recovery by serving locally grown, fresh produce. Eventually, she could expand and extend the offerings beyond the borders of Marin. If things went well with the diner, the news would spread to other eateries in the area. *'It'll require some strategic planning but it could work. This could be the last personal garden I grow. The meeting with Josh was timely.'* She thought. *'Soon water will be in greater supply and with better rates to support a resurgence of agriculture in the area.'*

She finished by mid-morning. On her way home, she picked up the latest issue of the Farin' and tossed it on the kitchen table without looking at it. She sat down at the table a short time later after showering and flipped the paper over to read the headline. There was another photo of the fire. A closeup of a diner window shortly before the wall fell. There was a faint indistinguishable gray blur in the window. The photo caption read,

What's in the window? What does it look like to you?

Found By the Water

This time she had to confront Brea and the Farin' editor in person. She poured herself iced tea, started the call for an appointment, and stopped after hearing a car door shut in her driveway. She opened the front door before her guest could ring the bell. Curiosity turned into incredulity as she saw who was there.

Anna watched Meg step awkwardly on to the porch. She appeared flushed and nervous after seeing the expression on Anna's face. Meg looked her full in the eyes. "Good morning. I'd like to talk to you if you have time now."

"Are you here to criticize me again?" Anna asked.

Meg shook her head. With a lopsided smile and pointing to the porch chairs, she replied, "No. I'd appreciate it if we could sit down for this conversation. Could we please?"

Anna locked eyes with her for a moment, nodded and led the way into her kitchen instead. "Have a seat Meg. May I get you some iced tea? I've fixed a glass for myself."

"That would be great, thank you," Meg replied.

"What's this about? The last time I saw you, you left me with the distinct impression you wouldn't care if we ever met again."

"The last time," sipping tea to sooth her dry mouth, "I was inexcusably rude and mean to you. I was wrong."

Hiding her astonishment, Anna responded. "I don't understand."

"The Lord used a friend and some bible verses to convict me that I was unjust and harsh in the way I reacted. I know you are not responsible for Glen's collapse, and I am sincerely sorry for my behavior."

"To be honest, I can't fathom where all your anger, the force of your attack, came from. What have I done to cause you to dislike me so much?" Anna asked.

Meg squeezed a lemon slice into her glass and stirred in sugar. "You haven't done anything, Anna. This is entirely on me. When we were young, I watched your life with envy. You had everything money could buy. You never hung-out with us after school. Your last name was Marin." Meg's face reddened slightly. "I felt inferior to you. I created this idea you thought you were too good for us, that we were unworthy of your friendship. It was unfounded, but it has colored all my impressions of you since. Then when you became Council Chair, I blamed you every time Glen came home tense from a meeting. I realized this week that I never

92

Found By the Water

took the initiative to get to know you. That's not the way God wants me to live. I sincerely ask you to forgive me."

Silence followed the confession, before Anna responded. "The truth is I'm never comfortable in social situations. I had responsibilities at home because my parents worked long hours which is why I kept to myself. I admit I did get more handed to me than some people, materially anyway. But social interaction has never come naturally. I learned to do what I had to do in the most efficient manner possible. Taking control of situations helped me do that. My parents rewarded hard work and results, not what they referred to as frivolity."

"You never really had a chance to have a childhood, did you? I hope you will accept my apology and we can start again. I'd like to introduce you to some women who would welcome the chance to befriend you. What do you say?" Meg held out her hand with a smile.

Anna took the offered hand and nodded. "I accept your apology. But I need a chance to think about our conversation." She stood, signaling the end of the visit. "Thank you for coming, Meg. Now, if you will excuse me, I need to take care of some urgent business. How is Glen? Have you seen him today?"

"He's recovering and will be home earlier than we expected. He's in a private room now. I'll see him again tomorrow."

Meg left Anna's house feeling subdued. But she knew she had done what God wanted her to do. She would leave it to him to work in Anna's life.

Chapter 27

Not circulate a false report. Exodus 23:1

Anna grabbed her car keys and both copies of the Farin' as soon as Meg drove away. After calling the editor and learning that the contributor of the latest offending submission was Brea as before, she headed to the hospital. When Anna had threatened legal action against the paper, the editor agreed not to print any further unsubstantiated and inflammatory material.

Anna knocked on Glen's door and heard the familiar gravelly voice. She peeked into the room. He opened his eyes and took a deep breath when he saw her.

"Hi Anna," he said pointing to the Farin'. "I've been expecting you."

"Hi." She replied tentatively. Then blurted out in a gush of words, "I'm glad you are well enough to leave ICU. What would we do in Marin without you?"

"Well Anna, I imagine you'd manage but it's nice to hear you say that." Glen smiled. "Why don't you sit down and we can talk about this article?" He waved toward the chair to his left.

Complying, she said, "You mean both inflammatory articles, don't you? I called the editor."

"I only saw the photo from one issue. There were others since then?" He took the issue she held out. "What did the editor say?"

Anna's face tightened. "It was Brea. She must have been standing directly behind us. These are her insinuations. Do you remember what I said to you at that moment? I know things were intense at the time."

Glen thought for a bit and said, "'What's that in the window?' Isn't that what you asked? The next second the window was gone."

Anna nodded. "I did see movement but wasn't sure if it was smoke or something else. I think I should talk to the inspectors. Their reports indicated nothing out of the ordinary."

Found By the Water

"I called them a couple days ago. They reviewed everything again and there was nothing. It must have been smoke you saw. The bigger issue is what are we going to do to stop the incriminations." Glen looked exhausted.

"I told the editor we'd take legal action if it continued. That should stop him. It's Brea I need to talk with next. I'm sorry to bring this trouble to you. I didn't know who else to ask. Thanks for talking to the inspectors. You don't think we missed anything, do you?"

"No, Anna, I do not. I hope your call to the editor puts an end to all this." He closed his eyes for a moment and was immediately asleep. Anna left quietly wondering what was fueling Brea's treachery.

Chapter 28

A heart that devises wicked plans. Proverbs 6:18

Brea waylaid Sean in the corridor coming out of his father's office. "Hey Sean, do you have a minute?"

"Five minutes tops. I'm on a mission for Dad." He kept walking.

"That's what I want to talk about," she replied, following him. "Care to grab something in the breakroom while we talk? It'll be empty this time of day and I could use some caffeine." Barely containing his impatience, he turned in at the door.

After they were seated, he looked at Brea expectantly.

"My idea for stalling the Marinetas is progressing. Josh was in Marin because it's been the hardest hit economically." She paused for effect. "He met with the Council and laid out his strategy."

"Dad learned that at a recent CVWA Board meeting." Sean countered impatiently. "Was the Council receptive or not?"

"At first, they weren't, after some well-timed comments from me. In the end they decided to join forces with him. They voted for Glen Stuart, the Fire Chief, to be Marin's Council representative on the CVWA Board." Brea took a sip. "Isn't your father a long-time member of the Board?"

"Not anymore. He resigned from it and his CVWA employment."

"I never understood why he continued to work there anyway." She commented.

"Because it kept him informed on the water policies." He replied curtly. "You know my family depends on the water supply to support our livelihood. But he can see that there's no stopping the Marinetas from that quarter. He's working on another angle." Irritated, Sean stood up abruptly when he saw Brea's keen interest in the last piece of information.

Found By the Water

"Brea, I've spent too much time already. I have to get going." Sean pushed his chair toward the table. "I'll pass on your information to Dad. Good work."

"Sean, there is one more thing I want to tell you."

"Not today Brea. I don't have time."

After Sean left, Brea refilled her coffee cup and sat back down. *'Just as well. It'll give me more time to stir things up for Anna.'*

Chapter 29

Two are better than one. They have a good reward for their labor.
Ecclesiastes 4:9

Eric stuck his head around the door of Glen's hospital room. "Hey Glen. I hear you're well enough to go home in a few days. Are you up for a short visit?"

"Eric. You bet I am! I haven't had the chance to thank you properly. I heard it was your idea to open the headgates a week before the fire. Don't know how to express my gratitude. It was huge! If you hadn't done it, all of Main Street would have been destroyed and there would have been nothing we could do."

"It was a timely decision, that's for sure. Who could have known how it would play out? You can thank Josh, and Rob too."

"I had heard that from Anna Marin. In a recent Council meeting with Josh, he made so much sense, even Anna came around."

"Rob and Josh are different. That's why I came today. I think you and I have a lot in common. Firefighters. Both of us Chiefs. You, for years. We care about our communities. Would you be interested in joining forces to revamp both our departments' policies and practices? I can see us focusing on everything from optimal water levels and safety measures to budget overhauls, equipment needs, training and everything else we oversee."

A spark of light flashed in Glen's eyes as he listened. "From what I saw as we fought that blaze, I'd be happy to collaborate with you. Until recently, I've been fighting a losing battle with no sign of things changing. I told Anna, the Council should at least listen to Josh, before forming any opinions. I'm glad she did. He's a clear thinker. Let's talk more when I get home and I'm cleared to go back to work. Are you going to leave the water levels as they are? Did you hear that I will be Marin's representative on the CVWA Board? Life just keeps getting better."

Found By the Water

"I hadn't heard but I'm glad. Best decision Marin could make. Yes, levels stay the same until negotiations with Marin are completed." Eric said smiling. "Hope you're back to work quickly."

"I've been wondering how I can live with the stress of my job, council dynamics, the water shortage and what would have happened without your intervention. I've been ready to quit and go back to plumbing. I still do some, you know. I never dismantled or sold my company. But the Lord must want me on the Council for a reason. He cares about Marin and so do I. Your proposal is an answer to my prayers. Who would ever have known Anna could change her mind, as well!"

"I'm also a believer, Glen. Rob and Josh are more like family to me than my own. I trust them with my life. They have been praying for years about better customer relationships with CVWA. At first, I was skeptical but I see God answering. He's an expert at softening hardened hearts. He must be if he got through to me." Eric said.

"I know what you mean. He's patient, never gives up his pursuit of us." Glen said. "Do you want to pray with me? Let's ask God to show us how to move forward. There's more going on than we know. There are lives he wants to turn around to himself. We'll need his wisdom and grace if we're going to succeed." Glen's eyes stayed shut when Eric opened his. A smile was still on Eric's face when he climbed into his car and called Josh about the new joint fire readiness review team.

Chapter 30

Every good and perfect gift is from above. James 1:17

Driving to Bellalto to meet Rob and Josh for dinner, Anna considered the events of the last couple of months. So much had changed since the morning in her garden, bemoaning her life. Matt had removed himself from her home. Water levels in the river had risen at no cost. She had met some nice people. All except Meg. Anna had accepted her apology but she was not ready to be too friendly. And the fire; but it seemed that some good would come out of that tragedy. It would have been worse if it had not been for Josh and Rob. She could almost believe they had no ulterior motives. It seemed she was beginning to trust them. *'I'll learn more tonight. Then I'll know.'* She reassured herself silently.

She had asked to meet them at the restaurant on the lake so she could leave if she felt the need. The lake shone like glass in the absence of a breeze. Both men stood up as she arrived at the table.

"Hi Josh. You must be Rob."

"Hi Anna. I'm happy to finally meet you." Rob put out his hand and smiled. "Thank you for joining us tonight. Regrettably, it was a long time coming." He sat down after her.

"Rob, I've been looking forward to thanking you for your part in saving Main Street during the fire by opening the headgate. Josh assures me you are different than your father and the long line of Marinetas. I hope that proves to be true." Anna said straightforwardly.

"I hope that's your conclusion too, Anna. Why don't we order and start learning about each other?"

They talked about Anna's childhood and what it was like to have such an enduring legacy in the area. She was surprised to experience an unfamiliar longing. *'They genuinely care about me.'*

As they finished the meal, Rob asked, "Anna, would you care to have dessert on the patio overlooking the lake? There is more to tell you about the history of this region. I think you'll be happy if you do." Rob spoke casually belying the importance of the moment. Josh was watching Anna closely.

She looked from Rob to Josh, then back to Rob. She studied their faces, finding them sincere and welcoming.

"Alright. I have an hour, Rob, before I need to be home. I have a lot to do tomorrow."

They gathered around the table waiting for their coffee and cobbler that was a restaurant specialty. Anna felt comfortable, as if she'd known them for years.

Rob had an old book on the table next to him. "Anna, I have a story to tell you. Are you aware that my wife Rebecca, Josh's mother, grew up in the valley area?"

"No, Rob. It must have been hard after more than a century of ill will toward those of us who live in the valley. How well did that work out?"

"Rebecca was the love of my life. My father was not at all happy about the relationship. Rebecca, to her credit, loved my father and in time he grew to love her. But the early years were hard for her. I didn't fully understand the bad feeling between the mountain and valley people until I met her. Nothing I heard had prepared me for the depth of it. I've never been one to follow blindly. Josh is the same way. For us, it became a personal challenge to not prejudge people." He looked at Anna and smiled.

"When I was a young man, I was introduced to Jesus Christ by some friends. I saw something different about their lives than the other people around me. I asked a lot of questions. I read the bible they gave me and listened while they patiently explained. I met my Rebecca through them. I eventually knew that Jesus loved me and gave my life to him. It was another thing my father didn't understand." Anna shifted in her chair as she listened.

"Did you bring me here to convert me?" Anna asked nervously.

"I'm just telling my story, Anna." Rob said kindly. "One day after my father became ill, I was searching the attic for family records. It had so much crammed into it I almost missed this old journal. When I started to read it, I understood the source of all the regional animosity. Would you like to read some of it tonight?" Rob handed her the journal. Stalling, she took a spoonful of dessert.

Found By the Water

"Is there something specific you want me to know? What does an old Marineta journal have to do with me?"

"Because I learned we're family; you, me, and Josh. We're overjoyed by it. An ancestor of ours wrote this journal. This is her personal account of what happened after her father and uncle had a disagreement. A great rift entered the family. She was heartbroken because she loved them all. Have you ever heard this story, Anna?"

Shocked, she sat stiff and silent. Her first thought was, *'I'm not alone. I have a family and it's the Marinetas of all people!'*

She answered cordially, hiding the swirl of emotions. "I heard some of this from Josh at the Council meeting. I had no idea at the time that it related to me personally. If this is true, why haven't you told anyone before now?"

"Because my father wouldn't have changed even with this knowledge. He was the Marineta leader, as well as for much of Bellalto. It would only have hurt you to know this sooner and not be able to assuage the pain that it might cause you. I didn't want to harm you in anyway. I've been praying for the right time. To be honest, you haven't exactly been open to getting to know us either."

"How do I even know this book is authentic?" Still not willing to acquiesce.

"You'll know when you read it. Will you read a little tonight?" Josh asked quietly.

Reluctantly, not wanting to be rude, Anna drew the book toward her and opened it. Tears came suddenly. "The author's name is Elianna Marineta." She said softly, not looking up.

Chapter 31

God sets the solitary in families. Psalm 68:6

Anna turned to the first entry; then flipped to the middle of the journal. She read:

March 20, 1860 Today I made another visit to Uncle John's home in the tiny settlement of families that left Bellalto. They are talking of village status and naming it Marin. Uncle is so ashamed of the disgrace Father has brought to the family name that he has legally changed his to Marin. He is giving his new name to the village because he thinks of himself as the leader in the valley. They are two peas from the same pod. My aunt and cousins support him but they are understandably lonely for the close bonds we all used to share. I talked to both men about forgiveness. That we all have areas of our lives that do not line up with scriptures. If we want to live in a Godly way, we must learn how to humble ourselves and admit where we are wrong. Uncle is still so angry he will not hear me. Father will not either. Since I last visited, I can see that Father's way of withholding water to those regions is causing hardship. The water levels are too low to allow the community to thrive. Lord, will you please show them the error of their ways and how to work together for the good of all of us?

Anna's parents had not told her much except that her ancestors had made their home in the valley in the mid-nineteenth century. She looked at Rob and Josh, hiding her true emotions.

"Yes, I'd like to read the journal. How can I do that? I imagine you don't want to let it out of your hands."

"We made a copy for you. This is yours. If you want to check anything with the original, feel free to ask us." Josh handed her a binder with her name on the cover.

"Could I have a few more minutes to read the journal's last entry?"

"Take all the time you want." Rob gestured to the waiter to refill their cups.

The last journal page puckered in several places and the ink was blotched, as if by tears.

Found By the Water

February 24, 1883 This journal has recorded my deepest longing for many years. I am an old woman now and ready to meet Jesus. God has graced my life with love, joy, and the knowledge of his Son. I will not be the one to bring reconciliation to my beloved mountains and valley. Father and Uncle left a legacy of bitterness that permeates the entire region. Lord, I will be with you before long, face to face. I see now that it was your purpose that I pray and work toward reconciliation. I have been faithful. Since I know you heard my prayers, it is clear to me that you have a different plan for someone to come after me. They will be the one you will use to bring harmony to this land. Thank you, Lord. I will see you soon with great joy.

Anna closed the book gently. Rob and Josh saw conflicting thoughts and emotions cross her face. It was too early to press.

"We have one more thing to give you tonight that may help you feel more comfortable about this news. It's Josh's and my DNA results from one of those find-your-family sites. You may want to send for your own. We're certain we're all related to Elianna and her family. We, on her father's side and you, on her uncle's."

She swallowed her emotions and nodded, taking the report.

"Anna, could we pray before you leave? This is a lot to absorb. We believe that God has several intentions for us. One is the very personal reason of being a family. Another is to bring the region into harmony. We three are the 'someone after' Elianna prayed about."

"I don't pretend to understand. I'm starting to trust you which doesn't come easy for me. So, yes, it's okay for you to pray."

"Lord, thank you that Anna, Josh, and I are a family. It is a wonderful thing you have done. You heard Elianna's prayers. You hear ours now, having set us about this work. Guide us into a deeper understanding of you. Show us how to accomplish your purposes. We love you. Amen."

"Well, thanks. I'll be heading home now. I need time to absorb all this information. Thank you for dinner and the journal. I enjoyed myself."

"This is a momentous occasion, Dad, for all of us." Josh said after Anna had left.

⁓

Driving home, Anna prayed, "God, I asked you a while ago if you cared about me. I'm beginning to believe that you do. Show me more." Even though the revelation tonight seemed too good to be true, she was surprised to realize that she wanted to belong in this family.

The next morning, her priority was to send for a DNA analysis and for the creation of her family tree.

Chapter 32

Pray without ceasing. 1 Thessalonians 5:17

Glen kept his focus on the road. "I'm enjoying being able to drive again." It had been a week since the Council meeting. Meg had agreed with Glen's appointment as Marin's representative to CVWA. "It was a good idea you had for a long weekend at the inn, Meg. It's the perfect spot to relax and enjoy nature before the craziness of normal life begins again." They planned to head back home on Sunday for Glen's first day back to work on Monday morning.

Nestled into a clearing upriver from Lake Chute, the views were lovely. Water bubbled in a stream alongside the main lodge of Mountain Hideaway B&B. With crisp mountain air wafting in, they were quickly asleep.

Saturday dawned a perfect day. Easy walking paths cut through the woods in several directions. They took leisurely walks each day and dinner in the renovated carriage house.

"I wish we could stay longer," Glen said. He took a deep breath with closed eyes. "I feel so relaxed right now. Thinking about going back to work has me a little anxious. I admit it's not as bad as it could have been considering the changes that are coming."

They were silent for a few moments. Glen finally said, "I have a lot to seek the Lord about. I don't think I've done a particularly good job when it comes to the Council. I need to pray a whole lot more. Will you help me?"

Leaning over to give Glen a hug, Meg assured him she would. "I think we should have dinner a little earlier on meeting nights. That way we can spend some time praying before you leave. What do you think?"

Glen grinned. "I think that would go a long way toward lowering my stress level. I don't have to do this all on my own. God will help me if I allow him to." They returned home Sunday refreshed.

Chapter 33

Death and life are in the power of the tongue. Proverbs 18:21

B rea's boss at the Farin' stood in front of her desk. "Look at all the letters that have arrived since your campaign began to garner public opinion for ousting the Mayor. Circulation is up slightly."

"I wasn't aware there were that many. I've seen a couple. Why weren't they placed in my inbox?" Brea grabbed for them irritably.

"I asked to see them first so I could monitor reactions. After Anna's call, I'm making sure we're on solid ground before proceeding. If we don't have the town behind us, it won't go anywhere. I'm taking a risk with this idea of yours." He laid the letters on her desk. "Let's print some in tomorrow's issue."

"Yes, sir." She replied, thinking, *'Do I need to work on a different angle? I expected more of a response from Anna by this time.'*

As Brea read the letters, she could see some were from the usual curmudgeons. Readers would discount anything they wrote. She created a brief lead-in to draw attention to two letters, from more influential readers, to print on 'The Editor's Desk' page.

We have heard you! The Farin' is flooded with letters protesting the lack of information. Should there be an investigation into the allegations of a Mayor's cover up related to our recent disaster on Main? Send your opinions to the Editor's Desk, c/o How's Marin Faring 215 Main Street or email to howsmarinfaring.com.

'Now I'll wait.' Brea knew how to be patient.

Chapter 34

All scripture is given by inspiration of God and is profitable.
2 Timothy 3:16

Dani put down the Farin' with disgust. She was in the building site office of her current project.

"Did you see the latest from the newspaper editor?" She said to the job foreman as she stood up to leave, picking up the paper. "What's the matter with those people? I'll check back on progress later."

Reaching her car, she called Anna before pulling out and left a message.

"Anna, hi. This is Dani. Would you like to get together for lunch again today? I'll meet you at your office. See you soon. I'm heading over now."

Anna was working at her desk having decided on a plan of action. Her idea for the town helping the Bolton's was a good one. All she needed was the Council's input and approval. That meeting was tonight. She didn't realize that her excitement showed in her face until she looked up at Dani's knock on the door frame. She was smiling too.

"Hi Dani." Anna greeted her.

"Anna, you look happy." Dani replied. A delicious aroma filled the room from the large bag she carried. "I brought lunch from my favorite barbecue place. Interested?" She set the bag on Anna's sofa table and began placing containers on it.

"Mac's BBQ! It smells so good. What made you think of me?" Anna sat in the upholstered side chair next to Dani.

"I was reading the Farin' and you came to mind." She gave Anna a searching look. "Have you seen it today?"

"No but I've seen the other two innuendos Brea submitted. I talked to her and the editor. I thought they'd stop this nonsense by now." She took a bite. "What was today's about?"

Found By the Water

"Here. You can read it for yourself." Dani placed the paper in front of Anna. "Let's enjoy our lunch before you read it."

"Good idea. Tell me about the bible study your friend mentioned last time we had lunch together."

"We're learning how to apply timeless lessons to our lives today. Have you read the bible?" Dani asked.

"No. I've been in churches for weddings and funerals. Why is it important that ancient writings be relevant today?" Anna asked.

"For a lot of people, they help us understand God better. We can read words he inspired other believers to write long ago so every generation would know him."

"Would you give me an example of something he said that is relevant today?" Anna was being drawn in.

Dani was quiet for a moment. "This verse came to mind just now. It's one of my favorites. 'I have loved you with an everlasting love. I have drawn you with unfailing kindness.'[8] There was a time when I didn't believe in God. During a hard time in my life a friend talked to me and I wanted to know more." She paused.

"Do you believe God loves you?"

"I know he does. Do you?" Dani replied.

"No. Honestly, I don't. I haven't thought about it until recently. On a particularly discouraging day not long ago, I was worried as to what I could do to alleviate the water problem. But you know how it is. Soon I was reviewing my entire life. Then I heard myself wondering aloud if God saw me and the difficulty I was having. I don't exactly know why I thought of him at that time because I never have before. I guess it was because I'm at my wit's end about some things and it would be good to know I wasn't alone." Anna took a breath. "Maybe I've said too much."

"If we're honest with ourselves, we all come to that point, eventually." Dani offered. "Talking to God is a good starting point. I remember when I thought I had all the answers and could handle life on my own. I learned the hard way that it wasn't true. And I'd like to help you Anna, in any way I can."

"I-, excuse me." Anna stopped when she heard her phone ring. "Hello. This is Anna Marin."

"Hi Josh. I'm at lunch with Dani right now." She glanced at Dani for her reaction and received a smile in return. "I'll ask."

112

Found By the Water

"Dani, Josh wants to give me a history lesson about the origins of Bellalto. Are you open to riding out there with me? He said it would take no more than two hours. It might help us both to know about our neighbors."

"I have the time. It sounds interesting." Dani began gathering the remains of their lunch.

Chapter 35

I will do a new thing. Isaiah 43:19

Driving to Bellalto, Dani and Anna continued the conversation started over lunch. "How did you meet Josh, Dani?"

"Through some business associates when I first moved here. It wasn't long before I learned we had a mutual friend in Eric Miller." Dani replied. "Turn here, it's a short cut. I've been to the house many times since Eric and I started dating.

"What's your story, Anna? Is there anyone special in your life?"

"No. I haven't had a great history with men after my husband died. I recently broke up with someone I was living with because I realized I get involved for all the wrong reasons. I have unresolved issues related to my family." Anna replied. "Speaking of family, did you know that the Marinetas and I are related? Josh wants to show me where it all began for our families a long time ago."

"I didn't know that. How long have you known?"

"I learned it recently on the night I met Rob at the Lakeside restaurant. There's an old family journal that I've started to read. I'm still trying to absorb the facts because my family has hated the Marinetas forever and I'm ambivalent about the news." Anna said. "I am happy to learn I have a family and I'm not alone anymore. I'm also working through all I've been told and know about them, although Rob and Josh seem different than past generations."

"His driveway is just ahead at the end of the cul-de-sac. I'm happy for you Anna. I can't wait to see what Josh is going to show us." Dani said as she and Anna stepped out of the car. Josh came out the door to greet them.

"Dani! It's good to see you again. Anna, glad you could come today." He led the way to a path behind the house. "This land belongs to my family. It's also the birthplace of Bellalto and the entire region.

Found By the Water

"That's why I want you to see it. As we begin working to unite the area and improve relationships, I thought it would be meaningful to see the old homestead land where the first Marinetas and others lived their early years, both your branch, Anna, and mine before the rift."

They entered the darker coolness and Anna breathed deeply. The stillness and the earthy green scent were a balm to her soul. The three walked along in companionable silence lost in their own thoughts. Anna felt as if she were waking from a deep sleep. There were more connections to these mountains than she had ever dreamed of.

Dani broke the silence. "Josh, Anna told me about the journal Rob found and that you're related. Is that why you've started your customer relations project in Marin?"

"No, it was because we saw the economic need there. It probably would have been easier to start somewhere else." He said with a smile for Anna.

"I'm finding it hard to absorb that we're cousins, long removed." Anna confessed.

"And Josh, you knew nothing about the Marin connection until you had the journal?" Dani asked.

"I was stunned. When I asked Grandfather if he had known about our familial roots, he only said it was history and better left that way. I became angry. History and connections to the past have always been important to me. It drove a bigger wedge between us."

"I know you weren't close with Mike. Eric has mentioned a few things."

"When I was a little boy, we were. He was happy for me to play on his study floor as he worked. He had no interests other than work and water. When I grew older, he thought I should be more like him. He said I was like my Dad, thinking I knew better than all the generations that had come before. It was the water that mattered to him, a family obligation and responsibility. Nothing came before it."

"What did you do?" Anna asked.

"I talked with Dad about it a lot. I was happy to be like him. His heart is so wide it draws people in. He thinks more about others than about himself. My Mom was the same way. He learned early not to fall into his father's unhappy way of life. After he came to know Christ and trust him with his own life, Dad learned even more about his calling. It is to unite the valley and mountain people. It put him at greater odds with Grandfather. They loved each other, I'm sure, but didn't agree on the important things in life. Dad was always respectful of his father but spoke from his own convictions. He had to wait to start working on God's vision."

"Your grandfather sounds a lot like mine and my parents. I've tried to live up to their expectations, being a Marin and all that goes with it. How did all this affect you?" Anna replied.

"For a while, I began to second guess myself. My Dad has spent a lot of time fostering a sense of my own God-given purpose. I still struggle though at times when I feel like I fail to achieve a goal."

Anna nodded. "I know what you mean. You had Rob to help counterbalance Mike's expectations. My family sounds a lot like Mike. I tried hard to be who they wanted me to be. And I've realized lately that I still try to be like them; still needing their approval. At least you didn't do that."

"You know," Josh said, "It sounds like a similar type of life view passed from generation to generation. Dad and Mom had the courage to start a new legacy; to be agents of reconciliation."

"Dani, Anna and I have a mutual ancestor, Elianna, who prayed for reconciliation. I believe we are the generation that God has appointed to bring lasting peace to this region. You're included. Your business takes you all over the area. You could be an emissary of goodwill too."

They had been walking steadily up a steep incline for half an hour while they talked. The path evened out suddenly into a broad meadow. Tombstones were visible on the far side. The view was spectacular, breathtaking even, with the roar of turbulent water falling nearby.

"What is this place, Josh?" Anna asked quietly.

"It's our family cemetery. I didn't realize we were coming this way. We missed the path that leads to the homestead while we were talking. But I like to think that this is where our ancestors fell on their knees after the long climb and cried out "Bella!"

As they walked across the meadow, Anna gazed at the vista before her. She understood exactly what the first Marinetas had felt so long ago. There were many family plots, marked by low drystone walls. There were grand monuments and more modest memorials. She saw that some stones had pitted with age and were dark with years of weathering; hard to read.

Found By the Water

Some were cleaner than others. It looked to be a work in progress. Unconsciously, she brushed her hand across the monument closest to her. Some of the moss fell off and she bent down to read the name. Startled, she said, "John Marin! What's a Marin grave doing way up here?" she asked shakily. "Is that Elianna's uncle?"

"As far as we have determined, yes, it is. We are uncertain how it came about. The journal said nothing about it. His wife's and children's graves are here, too."

Something new resonated through her like a strong current. It was a sense of connection. What she said next was far more practical.

"Dani and I have to be getting back if I want to be on time for the Council meeting. Glen's attending in person and we have some important issues to discuss. Can we go to the old settlement another time?"

"Sure. Dani, you might find the old building foundations interesting. You're welcome to join us. And Anna, the Council is invited as well. Ask them tonight and call me."

Chapter 36

Live in harmony with one another. Romans 12:16

The Council members gathered, including Glen who was now home. Anna shook hands and greeted them with a smile.

"Thank you for coming tonight. Glen, we are happy to have you back and recovered. We owe you and your crew a debt of gratitude for saving Main Street." Voices around the table confirmed the mutual feeling. "There are some important decisions to be made tonight. Does anyone mind if we table the other items until the next meeting?"

"No Anna and thanks for the warm welcome." Glen spoke for all. "What's the topic tonight? Can we talk about the fire? We couldn't have done it without the support from Josh, Eric and the Valley crews."

"We will. It was the worst event in Marin's recent history. We have a lot to talk about. Can we talk about the diner first?" She looked at the group who nodded. "Okay. I am concerned with helping the Bolton's rebuild. They have received the insurance claim reimbursement and it's not enough to cover all the construction and furnishing expenses because they hadn't updated their coverage policy. I've been thinking about how to help them with the difference. That's what I'd like to talk about tonight."

They nodded in unison noting Anna's empathy and her asking for their opinion. "It was during lunch at the Wild River with Dani Evans that started me thinking of a way to help Gus and Jennie to give them a new start. I have some land outside town off the main route. It's in a pretty area with a lake view and mountains in the distance. It's near the river and a perfect place for a diner. I've already asked them about the financial outlay to rebuild. With the insurance money they received and a reasonable land purchase contract, there is almost enough funding to build there. Do you have any ideas for how the town could help them obtain the rest of the funding?"

Found By the Water

"There is the diner property. They could sell that and make up the difference." Brea said quickly, happy to be first with a great solution.

"That makes sense." Sally agreed. "Property values have held steady for several years."

"But whoever buys it will need a reasonable purchase price because they'd have to build something else there."

"Not necessarily. It could be repurposed without a building on it." Brea offered. "I've always thought green space in the middle of the shopping area would be a good thing but who would want to own it?"

There was silence as an idea took shape. Glen spoke. "Would the town be willing to consider buying the property and turning it into a park?"

Anna smiled from the relief of not doing this project alone. "Let's look at the numbers. I've prepared a folder for each of you with last year's annual and this year's quarterly financials. Also, included is the cost of rebuilding on the new property out of town and the bank's appraisal of the old diner property. Then you can tell me what you think."

They worked steadily for a couple of hours before voting. All agreed the project was feasible, pending a report on the cost of turning the area into a public gathering place. A small committee accepted the task. They scheduled another meeting in two weeks for committee reports and a final vote.

"Anna, have you spoken to Gus & Jennie about this idea? Are they interested in rebuilding out of town on the new property?" Glen asked.

"I have and they are very excited about a new start." Anna replied. "I had to ask them before talking to you. Oh, and Evans Construction submitted a reasonable bid price. The Bolton's are planning to accept it and sign a contract this week. They may have done so already. Dani's crew will rebuild for them."

"Anna, you seem different tonight." Brea said.

"I have begun to realize how much I rely on all of you for the good of Marin. Your dedication and hard work show you care very much about doing the right thing for people. I'm sorry I've never told you how I felt. It's time I did. I'm working to change."

"We like it, Anna. You've always led us to good solutions but it's really good to be involved in the decisions." Jacob said. "Can we talk about how the meeting went with CVWA about our water usage requirements before we adjourn?"

Found By the Water

"The meeting with the Board and Council subcommittees went smoothly. The analysis of the facts didn't take long. They weren't surprised by the additional usage data we presented them. But we were surprised by the reasonable rates they brought back to us. We are working on the contract details now." Glen reported.

"The contract will be reviewed at our next meeting for which I've asked several key business leaders to attend. We need to get them involved." Anna reported. "And in a couple of weeks, Glen will be installed as Marin's CVWA Board representative. That's the most exciting thing about all these new developments. To have a voice in the process."

"Also," Glen continued, "Eric Miller, the Bellalto Fire Chief, and I are joining forces to improve the region's fire readiness response from the ground up. Knowing the risk factors will be assessed and mitigated regionally is a huge burden lifted."

The meeting broke up and most of them smiled as they shook Anna's hand on the way out. It felt good to be a team. Anna was hopeful as she walked home. *'Things are looking up. If I'm nicer to people maybe God will love me.'*

Brea lay in bed that night kept awake by bitter thoughts. It was worse than she thought.

'I have to do more to stop Anna from making a fool of herself. It's all too strange. What does Anna hope to gain? They'll try to take advantage of her and before you know it, they'll be running the show. Then when it becomes my time to lead the Council, it will be harder to take the control back.'

She had formulated another approach before falling asleep. One that might work, but first she had to talk to a few people.

Chapter 37

Love your neighbor as yourself. Mark 12:31

Saturday was the day Anna could relax from the pressures of her life. This morning, she was trying to make sense out of a disturbing dream she had dreamt in the early morning hours. *'I was driving along; I passed a graveyard and thought the tombstones needed dusting.'*

Shaking her head, Anna picked up the journal, took her light breakfast to the patio and began to read from the beginning. An hour later, she went inside for a refill. Her phone rang as the door closed behind her.

"Hi Anna. Dani here. We didn't have a chance to talk about the latest Farin' trouble directed at you."

"I had forgotten about it." Anna's optimism dimmed. "Come over now if you'd like." Anna refilled her cup and made a fresh pot of coffee. There was still time to read one more day of the journal.

> September 9, 1862 Today was Uncle John's birthday. We used to have such wonderful celebrations. Today there will be none. At least not with Papa and me. Papa has turned into a cold hard man. I have decided to call him Papa in my journal. It is the name I called him as a child. He does not even mention his brother anymore, as if he does not exist. It encourages me to read how Jesus came to earth to heal and restore us back to unity with himself and others. I become exhausted in my spirit at times. It would be easier for me to give up and accept that my family is torn apart. I cannot be complacent. If Jesus was willing to give his life to restore me to friendship with his Father in heaven, how can I give up? There is a better way I read about today in Ephesians 3. It is the way of the cross and turning from the bitterness around me. If Christ could endure the rejection and pain to make a way for me, I can trust him with my family. Lord, enable our minds to understand how immense, how wide, deep, and high your love is for us. Draw us to you and to each other by your life-giving power.

Anna could not move on to the next entry. She re-read the prayer and felt an unexpected longing. She had never heard of or experienced love the way Elianna wrote of God's. She heard a car pull in and opened the

Found By the Water

back door leading into the kitchen before Dani reached the porch, carrying a package wrapped in newspaper.

"Morning Anna." Dani smiled.

"Hi. What's in the paper?" Anna asked holding the door open.

"Pastry right from the oven. I wrapped the container in the Farin' to keep it warm. What's printed on it is not as pleasant."

"Let me see." She put plates on the table, poured the coffee, and transferred the pastry to a serving plate before opening the paper.

"What are you thinking?" Dani asked.

"I'm getting an idea of why Brea is doing this." Anna looked up. "She wants to be Mayor or Council Chair. Not sure which yet but she's trying to unseat me by stirring up public doubt about my character."

"Why would she do that?"

"Good question. But it's consistent with other behavior Glen and I have observed recently. She has said as much but I think there is another motive she is deliberately concealing." Anna put the paper down.

"Have you decided how you're going to handle the situation? It can't be ignored. Readers should know they're being manipulated. Those letters are from people I've done business with. They've always been reasonable and I know they care about what happens in Marin. If you don't mind, I plan to talk with them." Dani persisted.

"I've already spoken to Brea. She defended her actions and it didn't stop her. I need to have another conversation with Glen. By the photo, she implies he's involved in a cover up as well. It would help if you talked to people you know." Anna replied. "Meanwhile, there are so many other things to focus on. Were the Bolton's receptive to the bid package you presented them?"

"I met with them this week. They signed a contract for us to build. My specifications were closer to their vision than any other contractor. Next steps are to finalize the blueprint, obtain the permits and legal documents, finish the foundation, and enclose before winter. We can work the interior when the snow comes. They're still looking at properties. They said they looked at a lot for sale off the main road to Bellalto near the river. Is that your land?"

"Yes. It's been in my family for generations. I've been doing a lot of thinking about my life lately. Few people know when I earned my business degree, I also earned one in horticulture. It's my real passion.

Found By the Water

There are gardens on the land that the Bolton's are purchasing. I am seriously considering moving away from public service to a farm to table business on another piece of land I own. There are enough restaurants and other places around here I could supply. It will be possible now that the water issue is being resolved."

"Could Brea have found out and is hedging her bets?" Dani asked.

"No. You're the first person I've told." Anna confessed. "I won't do anything until Marin's new relationship with CVWA is stable. I made a commitment to Josh to also be an emissary with other valley towns."

"Speaking of Josh, I see you've been reading Elianna's journal. How far have you gotten?"

"On the journal page I read today, Elianna mentioned how her Dad wanted her to call him Father. It sounds like a formal relationship, as mine with my parents. We were never close." Anna replied.

"It must have been lonely, Anna. I believe God designed us to be in families for closeness, belonging, love and support."

Anna's eyes were sad. "I never let myself think about that." She replied honestly.

Dani saw how hard it was for Anna to talk about her family and changed the conversation's direction. "What was in the last entry you read?"

"Some things I don't understand. She wrote about God's love. How immense it is. It sounds too good to be true. I've never experienced it and my family never acted like they had either."

"You may not have realized it, Anna, but you have experienced it."

Chapter 38

Humble yourselves before the Lord. James 4:10

Anna asked, "What do you mean?"

"Well, let's start with something recent. Remember your reaction in the meadow? The sound of rushing water, clear mountain air, the sun's warmth, and the scent of the grass? Your involuntary response? Yes, I saw it in your face. You had a profound experience at that moment." Dani said.

"I did."

"That's a little of what God prepared for you to show you he exists and wants you to know him. He set something of himself in everything he created, to help us understand him better. Some of it is known through our senses. Some is hidden knowledge for us to search out. We see his nature revealed through science. But the best part of it all is how somewhere deep within us, we respond with a longing we cannot explain. Do you deny you felt the tug?"

"I felt a sense of belonging." She realized. "I've never belonged anywhere or with anyone quite like this. But I did in the meadow. I thought it was a family connection.

"Here." Giving Dani the last journal entry she'd read, Anna said. "Read this. What can you tell me about God's love like Elianna knew?"

"She's referring to a verse in the bible." Dani handed the journal back. She pulled out a small bible from her purse. "You can read it for yourself." She flipped to Ephesians 3. "Start reading in verse one. This is a book written by an early Christian leader."

"He is very certain." Anna commented when she finished.

"It is possible to know God in a deep personal way, Anna."

"How can I know?" Anna asked. "Meg professes to be a Christian and look how she treated me. Did I tell you she apologized?"

Found By the Water

"God loves you, Anna. He wants you to know and love him too. Since he is holy, recognizing the sin in our life and our need for him is the first step. That's what Meg did. She acknowledged the sin of misjudging you and asked you to forgive her for doing it."

"I've never done anything really bad. I'm a good person." Anna protested. "Why would Meg do that? Why would it be important enough to come to my house and humiliate herself like that?"

"*Humble* herself." Dani corrected gently. "Meg *humbled* herself."

"What do you mean?" she asked.

"She knew she had sinned by judging you. Sin is when we don't align ourselves with God's purity and holiness, in our actions, thoughts and motives. It's wanting to live our life our own way; believing the way we live is good enough. We think we have no need of him." Dani paused. "It keeps us from having a friendship with him. By thinking that his ways are wrong or worse, we give no thought to him as if he doesn't exist."

Anna was quiet. She thought of her disregard for anyone who depended on religion; how she had thought she needed a man in her life to define her. She always worked to get her own way and had all but refused Meg's apology.

Aloud she asked, "How can anyone meet those high standards?"

"We can't. That's the point. After the first humans declared their independence from God, he immediately had a plan to restore them. His plan today is the same. You see, sin is costly. Only a sinless person could pay the price. We can never redeem ourselves. He sent his son, Jesus Christ, to live a sinless life on earth to tell people who his father was and how to be reconciled with him."

"How did that work out?"

"It worked out like he meant for it to and still does, for those who believe. Some ridiculed and rejected his message, just like today. He upset their lives too much. One day they arrested him on false charges and beat him so badly, he was unrecognizable. He died nailed to a cross accepting our sins upon his own body. Then with power in him, he rose from the grave. By paying the price for our sins, he made a way for us to be united to his father. He is the only Way to a relationship with God." Dani paused again giving Anna time.

Found By the Water

"When we believe this and ask him to forgive us, we begin a new relationship with him. It is also when we begin to better understand the depth of his love for us."

"Is that why Meg had to ask me to forgive her? Is this what makes you all so different than most people I've met?"

"Meg *wanted* to." Dani emphasized. "Because she's experienced God's forgiveness for herself. I have too. We ask for and give forgiveness when our behavior requires it. Then we make amends to those we've wronged, where we can. It's the way of the cross; where we find, and he gives mercy."

"Does God really forgive you when you sin time after time? It must be hard to be perfect." She said cynically.

"Yes, he does." Dani answered, ignoring her comment about being perfect. That discussion was for another day. She glanced at the time.

"Why have I never known this? Why have I been so alone all my life?" Anna persisted. "If he cared so much, why did he leave me to find my own way?"

"Would you have believed it then?" Dani asked gently.

"Yes! Yes, I would have!" Anna snapped back.

Suddenly a memory came of a friend at college who had tried to talk to her of God. Her mouth opened and closed. God *had* told her, and she had wanted nothing to do with him at the time. She wondered how many other occasions he had reached out to her.

Changing the subject, she brought up her dream. "What could it mean?"

"It may have been prompted by our visit to your family's graveyard. I need to get going Anna. I'll talk to the people I know and settle them down about the alleged cover up. I'll pray the meaning of your dream becomes plain to you. Let's do this again soon."

Anna walked Dani to the door and stood for another minute. She wanted to read a bible for herself.

Chapter 39

You will find me when you search for me with all your heart.
Jeremiah 29:13

Anna made it to her office at the Town Hall in record time to pick up the ceremonial bible. She found it easily and wiped the dust off. As she rushed out the door, she almost ran into Glen and Eric coming up the steps.

"Oh, I'm sorry! Wasn't paying attention. How are you Glen? Eric?" Talking rapidly, she turned to walk away, trying to hide the bible. "I'm running late. Talk to you later."

"Better every day." Glen's gaze went to the book in her hand.

"Is that a bible you have there?" Eric asked.

"What?" Now annoyed, Anna kept walking without looking back.

"The bible. Isn't that the town's bible?" Glen smiled.

"What if it is, Glen?"

"I never thought of you as interested before. Be glad to help if you have questions."

Irritated, she composed her face and looked at them. "Good to know. Thanks. Got to get going. Enjoy the rest of your day." Sliding into her car and pulling away she thought, *'Yes, I have a lot of questions but I don't know what or how to ask yet.'*

"Eric, let's pray for Anna." Glen said as they sat down in his office. "Father, we know you are speaking to her and she's searching for truth. We ask you to remove every hindrance to knowing you. Amen."

At home, unaware of the powerful prayer, she opened the bible sitting at the kitchen table. She turned to the first section in Genesis and read that God had created the heavens, earth, including humans. He gave them purpose, provision, freedom and free will to choose if they would follow his ways. She saw how God sought them out in a garden when they chose not to and gave them a chance to turn back to him.

Found By the Water

She didn't understand it all but continued reading until the story of a woman named Hagar stopped her. Hagar had fled for her life and rested by a desert spring. She caught her breath reading Hagar's words in response to God's promise to provide for her; 'You are the God who sees me.'[9]

It was a direct answer to the question she had asked God not long ago. A tight place in Anna began to unfurl. She reached for a pen to mark the story. Remembering the bible didn't belong to her, she purchased her own online.

'God, if you saw Hagar, you must see me. What do I have to do for you to love me? I've ignored you all my life. I've been living my own way so long I don't know how to change.' Anna was becoming used to the impromptu prayers to a God she didn't know yet. But her new friends did and she wanted what they had.

Chapter 40

Lord, deliver me from men who plan evil things. Psalm 140:1

Josh looked up to see Rob standing in his CVWA office doorway. "Josh, do you have a minute? Let's grab a coffee and take a break by the river."

"Why don't we do this more often?" Josh said over the sound of the rapids. He waved to the people navigating them. "We haven't taken the time to raft in a while either. We should do that soon. Have some fun." He smiled at his Dad who wore a serious expression. "What's on your mind?"

"There's something you should know. I've held off until I knew something definitive. I didn't want the chance of anyone over hearing so that's why we're here." Rob replied. "You know the discrepancies you found during your research for our customer relations project? I told you I was discreetly following up on it. It's serious business. What do you know about the Pettrie's, Josh?"

"The normal stuff you learn growing up in the same town. A lot of people wonder why he worked for CVWA for so long. It's strange, don't you think?"

"Like you, I also suspected CVWA funds were being funneled elsewhere. After you voiced your suspicion, I escalated the investigation. Valley income doesn't match up with rates and usage reports. It's been going on for five years."

"And you suspect either Tom Pettrie or Mark Thompson? Mark's lifestyle doesn't support that theory. He told me recently he and his wife had been approved for a bank loan for their son's tuition."

"No, not Mark. I suspected it was Tom even with all his family's money. I've also wondered why he continued to work after inheriting."

"I talked to friends in law enforcement," Rob continued, "and engaged a forensic accountant who's had experience as an undercover agent. He's followed the evidence to Tom. But to build a more solid case, he hired on as one of Tom's personal security agents when the opportunity arose."

"How much?"

"Close to $2 million over five years. He was patient and took a small amount each month. He used a computer key to get past the encryption, which allowed him to precisely adjust the rates and deposits so the syphoning wasn't easily detected. That's why he continued working when he didn't need to. But he forgot a critical component of the cover-up process. This is how the discrepancies were found."

"And when he quit, your agent was able to see the change? How did he expect to get away with it after quitting?" Josh wondered aloud.

"He had an inside person set up to continue his work. She changed her mind after he wasn't around to bully her and came to me. She cooperated by obtaining the remaining data needed to arrest him for embezzlement."

"So, you have the forensic evidence and witnesses. Will she testify?"

"She will. There's more, Josh. Our agent has proof that Tom is planning to harm me in some way to stop our progress to share water more equitably. An arrest is imminent. I can't say anymore yet. I want you to be careful from now on until this is settled; and pray about it."

"Let's do it now. 'Lord, you know all things from the end to the beginning. Please make them clear and protect all involved. Turn Tom's heart to you and use this for good in his and his family's lives. Amen.'"

Chapter 41

What must I do? Believe on the Lord Jesus Christ. Acts 16:31-32

Anna's bible arrived quickly and she continued to read accounts of God's faithfulness. In the Psalms she learned God had seen her in her mother's womb and had been watching over her since then.[10] She hadn't yet found anything to do with Jesus. Standing to stretch, she called Dani. "Morning. This is Anna."

"Good morning. How are you?"

"Since we met last, I bought a bible. I've been reading and have more questions." She paused to contain her urgency. "Would you have time to spend with me this afternoon?"

"I'd love to. That will give me time to wrap some things up. Why don't you come to my house? See you soon," Dani said and gave her address.

Eager to learn more, Anna arrived five minutes early as Dani pulled into her driveway. "Right on time. I like that." Dani greeted her.

When they were seated on the patio, Anna swallowed and took a deep breath.

"I know God sees me." She said quietly, a smile lighting her face as she placed the bible on her lap.

"I read about some of the things you told me. But I've only been through the Old Testament. I must have missed the parts about Jesus. I brought my bible so you can show me."

"There are some references to Jesus in the Old Testament. They foretell about his birth, death, and resurrection. Jesus' life and teachings are in the New Testament which begins with his life on earth." Dani helped her find the first promises about Jesus in Genesis[11] and 2 Samuel.[12] They talked about them for a while. Then she showed Anna promises about Jesus fulfilled in the New Testament. [13] [14] [15]

Found By the Water

"You mean the Old Testament is more than a collection of stories about God helping people?"

"He does do that. And he is always working to bring us into relationship with himself. It's in the New Testament where you'll see Jesus more clearly." Dani led her to Matthew to read about his birth.[16]

"Jesus was God and man; being born of a woman and of God. That's why he could live on earth in all humanness but never sin. In speaking of himself, he said he always did what he saw his Father in heaven doing.[17] The books of Matthew, Mark, Luke, and John tell of Jesus from different vantage points. But they all agree. You might want to read those next. We can talk again when you do.

"After his death and resurrection, Jesus' apostles took the good news to the world by several different means. One way was through books and letters to the churches in different ancient cities, written by inspiration from the Holy Spirit as a method of teaching and encouraging them.[18] These are included in the New Testament. They teach us about how to trust him in every area of our lives. He's motivated by his love for us. For you."

Quiet for a few minutes, Anna asked. "I know that God wants me to know him. How can I become good enough?"

"Anna, there is nothing you can do to make him love you more. It's God's gift of grace[19] because it shows us his favor in that we can do nothing to earn it. Otherwise, we would become proud and boastful."

"That's hard to believe. I've had to meet other people's expectations before I received their approval. It's how the world is."

"Anna, I've only known you a short time but I have never seen you trying to earn anyone's approval." Dani said with a smile.

"That's because I gave up! I decided I couldn't live out all the competing ways of earning love and decided to live my way." That sounded so familiar, she stopped talking in utter surprise. "Oh no!"

"We all have Anna. Until we see ourselves as falling short in our way of living and know God loves us enough to show us a better way."[20] Dani replied.

"Still, it's hard to believe. Isn't this your expectation of me?"

"Well, you called *me* and you're asking *me* questions. What does that tell you? I've tried to explain my faith to you. But if you decide not to believe him, then Anna, that's your decision." Dani spoke kindly and paused. "I think you're really seeking him and afraid it's too good to be true; that you'll end up hurt and alone again." She took a breath and continued. "Why don't you talk to him as you read? Ask Jesus some of your questions."

Continuing gently, Dani said, "I'd like to suggest that you take stock of the premise you've based your life on so far and consider how it helped you reach for what you're searching for now. Compare your beliefs to what you read. Then determine if you want to continue down your old path or his. That might help."

Anna closed the bible on her lap. Her emotions and thoughts were tumbling around. Was she willing to consider that her motto, of doing it her way, was false? "What did you do to believe, Dani?"

Watching Anna's internal struggles reminded Dani of her own. She couldn't explain it in a scientific way, although some people believe because of what they understand of science. She only knew the moment she had accepted God's gift of forgiveness in Jesus Christ had changed her life. God had helped her to the moment of faith.

"Grace. It was God's grace that brought me to the cross to place my own life in Jesus' care." Dani finally said. "I'd love to pray with you Anna before you go. Will you allow me to?"

"Grace." Anna said, trying it out. "I've never heard of it."

"His grace is clearly shown in Jesus Christ. Compassion for the arrogant and broken people alike; the hurting and those unlovely in their stubbornness and self-reliance. It's his peace to the restless and spiritual sight to those who are so blinded by scientific explanations of life, they don't leave room for God to interact with them. When we make room for him, he helps us come to him in faith."

Absorbing Dani's last explanation, Anna replied. "I'd liked to pray if you don't mind.

'God, I know now that you have always seen me and you alone have brought me to this moment. I have been far from you and want to draw closer. Jesus, I believe that you are the only way to a relationship with God and everything about you helps me understand him better. Please forgive me for my sinful ways; for choosing to live my life without you. I accept the grace you give which cost you so much when you died on the cross. I accept the life you made possible for me to receive when you rose from the grave. I am so happy to be yours. Teach me about yourself."

Chapter 42

The Lord your God fights for you. Deuteronomy. 3:22

Full of thoughts of God's grace and the continual assurances that he loved her, Anna drove to the river's edge to her secret refuge. It was another plot of land that had been in her family for decades. The river, with its powerful flow, helped her think more clearly. Today, her project was to hang a hammock chair on a thick tree branch, facing the Bella Chute. She sat down to try it out and found it was just the right height for comfort. She leaned against the back and stretched out her legs on a fallen log. Thinking back to her tombstone dream, Anna thought about the bitterness started by people who were no longer living. *'I'm tired of living a dead way of life by perpetuating my family's unhappiness. I've made it mine without even thinking about it. My life could have been different if they had left a legacy of forgiveness. I want to change that. Public service was my parent's desire for me. Not mine. I'll need to decide soon on a resignation date.'*

Picking up the copy of the Marin Farin' she had with her, she opened it to see if the editor had kept his promise to not print any more of Brea's lies. He had not.

WHAT'S ANNA MARIN COVERING UP?

We have the photo of Anna pointing at the window right before the wall fell. She saw something. What was it? Have you seen the vagrant that was hanging around for a while? I haven't. Was a body missed in the investigation? If you think she's covering up something, email the Farin' Editorial Desk.

She almost stopped breathing. This time it was worse than any other.

Found By the Water

Her pulse sped up as she read the article. It was yellow journalism at its best. While she knew none of it was true, many others would not. She swiped tears from her cheeks, reaching for her phone. It rang as her fingers hovered over it. Then she saw that the call was from a neighbor, Bob, who had accused her on her front steps the night of the fire.

'No, not answering.' She thought. *'Jesus, please help me now.'*

As soon as the phone stopped ringing, it started again. Another call, then another and another. All from people who, she was sure, had already read the article. They would have nothing helpful to say to her. Frozen in her seat, she gazed at the water flowing by. This situation was not going to pass by as quickly as the river did. Then a call came from Glen Stuart. It was not as if he was a friend yet but he was a trusted Council member. She took a chance.

"Hello."

Glen heard the hesitation and came directly to the point of his call. "Anna, it's Glen. Have you seen the Farin'?"

"Not doing so well right now. I don't understand," she answered with a tearful hitch in her voice.

Glen had never known her to cry. "I don't either. I'm with Eric Miller. We're hoping you would let us come talk to you."

"I'm at a place by the river. It's my special place. I don't want to come back home at this moment. Would you be willing to come here? No one knows where it is and I'd like to keep it that way. If you come, can I trust you? There's a place to pull in so your car can't be seen from the road."

"Yes, you can trust us. We're picking up Dani on our way."

She gave them instructions, wondering what it was they had to say to her that would change the situation. Tears started falling in earnest.

Fifteen minutes later, she heard a car pull up and footsteps approaching. Without turning around, she said, "I'm glad you are here. I need your help."

"You need my help? That's interesting."

Anna turned quickly. "What are you doing here? How do you know about this place?"

"I know a lot of things about you, Anna."

"Brea, what are you talking about? Please leave!"

Found By the Water

"Not until we've had a little talk." Brea sat down at the other end of the log. "I see you've read the article. How does that sit with your plans to start being so nice to people?"

"I asked you what you're talking about, Brea? I thought this was behind us. None of it is true!" Anna said angrily.

"I'm not so sure about that. I was there when you mentioned something about seeing a pale face in the diner's upstairs window. No one has heard a thing about it since. It's been weeks. It sounds like a cover up if I've ever heard one!"

A car door slammed behind them. "Anna. Brea?" Glen nodded. Eric and Dani were right behind him. "Anna, I thought you were alone."

"Brea arrived a few minutes ago. I didn't know she knew about this place. She's the source of the rumors and the reason for the libelous items in the paper." She gave Brea a hard look.

Glen's expression became sterner as he saw Anna's stricken face. "Brea, explain please." He walked around the log to face her.

Brea drew back a little at his presence. She had not expected interference, and from Glen of all people. Anna had been tougher on him than anyone on the Council board. "Just telling it like it is, Glen. I see you brought back-up," glancing at Eric and Dani.

"That's enough Brea. I asked you to explain. Why would you start a devastating rumor about Anna? It's not true, in any case."

"I'd have thought you'd be grateful for Anna to be brought down a peg or two. When she was high and mighty, running the show, she was my kind of leader. Now she wants to involve everyone in the decisions. A strong will is what's needed to run the Council and this town. Nice has nothing to do with it!"

"That doesn't make any sense, Brea! What does that have to do with the trouble you've been stirring up in the paper? I'm asking you to leave us now. The four of us have a lot to talk about. We'll get back to you later. This is not over by any means. You'll have to answer for this slanderous scheme of yours."

"I'm not done either. You'll regret this Glen." Brea stood up head high, her back stiff and walked to her truck. She drove away with a confused look. She thought people would be grateful to be rid of Anna. She knew she could do a better job leading the Council.

Chapter 43

I will be found by you, says the Lord. Jeremiah 29:14

Anna's words came out in little bursts. "What was that about? She's strange!"

"A little off center, Anna. I didn't have a chance to look at the window. I asked my crew if they saw anything. Some said they had seen a quick gray flash moving across the roof top to the adjacent building but it was smoky back there and flames were shooting everywhere. Hard to see."

"Is it even possible that someone was in the building and perished in the fire?" The horror overwhelmed her.

"We know it's a lie. The fire investigators are experts. I called them again this morning to ask what they found, after re-reading their report which did not mention human or animal remains. They confirmed the same. Eric also had worked his way through the rubble before they came and he saw nothing either. He's been doing this for a long time. Her accusation has no basis."

Anna calmed down listening to Glen and sat in silence.

"You've done nothing wrong, Anna." Eric said quietly. "What do you think Brea meant when she said you're becoming nicer? What was that a reference to?"

Anna gave a quick glance at Glen, her cheeks reddening. She stumbled over the words. "Ok, then. I'll tell you." She confessed quietly, "I've wondered if I was nicer to people, then God might love me. So, I tried it at the last Council meeting." She shot another quick glance at Glen and looked out over the river. "Seems Brea would rather me be my old controlling self and she's the only person who ever looked up to me for being that way. Am I really that bad? She thinks if I'm out of the way, she has a chance at my job."

Found By the Water

"Anna, you're the most qualified of anyone I know to lead the Council. Sometimes you can be a bit abrasive, I admit. But your instincts, analysis of situations and solutions are accurate, more times than not. To be honest with you, most of us on the Council board would like you to include us in all those things, too. Otherwise, why agree to participate? We care about Marin as much as you do. But trying to be nicer to win God's favor is all wrong. He loves you Anna, as you are."

"I know that now. Dani explained God's grace to me. She's been teaching me what the bible says about Jesus. I've been reading it." She said, "Yes, I had the bible that day you caught me at the town hall."

"When did you become interested in seeking after God?" Eric asked.

"At the beginning of summer; an extremely low point in my life when I realized I was alone and powerless to help the town with the water issue. My current relationship was going nowhere and I felt worthless; exhausted emotionally. That was the day I asked God if he saw me. It wasn't even a conscious prayer. I haven't thought about God much; I was raised to depend on myself.

"It was the day your car broke down, remember Eric? The day before the diner fire. Since then, I've met some wonderful people. Glen, I feel I know you better. I've heard all of you talk about Jesus, learned how you worship God, help others, forgive, and seek forgiveness. Best of all I have a family! I belong in a family who cares about me! Did you know about that? It's overwhelming when I think about it." Her eyes widened in surprise. "I realize that these are the ways God answered my prayer. He did see me that day and every day since he's been showing me!"

"Yes, he has. He's been waiting for you to realize your need for him." Glen agreed. "I haven't heard about your family though."

"Rob and Josh are my family. The Marinetas. Can you believe it?" Her eyes filling with moisture again. "It's a long story for another day. But I will tell you that they are nothing like I've always been led to believe."

"That's amazing Anna. You're not as alone as you thought you were." Eric said. "Congratulations. I'm happy for all the good changes."

Chapter 44

I will never leave you. Joshua 1:5

Walking toward their cars, Glen said, "We need to pay a visit to the Farin' editor, Anna, to ask for a retraction and his resignation. Let's go there right from here. We can all pray tonight for the best way to approach Brea. I've always thought she was the quiet, kindly type. This whole thing is puzzling. But I've suspected all was not right with her for some time."

They were climbing into their cars when Brea drove back in. They climbed out and stood in a close group watching her approach them.

"Brea, this is a surprise." Glen took the lead. He positioned himself ahead of the others to meet her. "Why did you come back?"

With her eyes on the ground, she answered in a mumble.

"I'm sorry Brea. We didn't hear you. Would you care to come back to the log, sit down and talk about it?" Glen asked.

When she and Anna were seated as before, she took a deep breath. With her head down, looking at her hands in her lap she began. "I came back to apologize to Anna. All I can say is that I was scared when Anna changed." She heard an indignant sound from Anna but wouldn't look at her. "I know, but Anna you have to admit it was out of character for you. I've always looked up to you as a great leader. It felt like you were losing control."

Choosing her words carefully, Anna replied. "Brea, I would like to apologize for how I've led you to believe that a good leader doesn't listen to others. All it has done is isolate me. I have been unintentionally disrespectful to many people because I didn't understand. But a lot of things have happened recently that have shown me that there is a better way to relate to people and get a job done. I don't want my former behavior to influence you as being appropriate leadership."

Found By the Water

"Are you going to tell me next that you've got religion? What will happen if no one can agree on anything? Nothing will get done."

"This doesn't sound like an apology. Why did you really come back?" Glen interjected.

Brea said, "I don't know what to expect anymore. I've always fashioned myself after her out of admiration." Turning to Anna, she asked. "Why did you change?"

"I have admitted this afternoon that I tried to be nicer to people because I wanted God to love me. I have been on a quest to know I'm significant to him. Dani and a lot of other people I've met this year have helped me see that I've always mattered to God, and so do you."

"I've never given it much thought. I'll try to accept the change in you. I came back to say that and to tell you I went to the Farin' office and asked them to pull the story. I admitted in the full retraction that I was wrong so the town will know. I've stirred up a pot of fury about you. I'm sorry."

"That's the least you could have done, Brea. Thank you for retracting. Your scheme wouldn't have gone far anyway. We have sufficient proof there were no remains in the fire." Anna's phone interrupted.

"Hi Rob."

"Anna, I'm calling to ask you to be careful. A situation has occurred that indicates you might be in danger." Rob spoke gravely.

"I'm with a few people right now so I'm good." Anna assured him.

"And there is someone on your Council who we believe is working with these factions to stop our agreement from moving forward. Her name is Brea Duncan."

"I see." She spoke tersely, looking at Brea. "That explains a lot of things. Anything else Rob?"

"Yes. An arrest is imminent here in Bellalto. Tom Pettrie. Computer crimes, embezzlement charges and solicitation to commit a crime of violence. Please call me back as soon as you're alone. I'd like to explain the circumstances to you."

"Is this information confidential or sharable?"

"It'll be public knowledge within the hour in Bellalto so, I'd say yes. Share it selectively if you have reason to believe someone else is in jeopardy. Be careful."

Brea moved uneasily as Anna hung up turning towards her.

Found By the Water

"That was an illuminating call. I learned that an arrest is occurring within the hour in Bellalto. Related to someone connected to Bellalto Rafting." Anna watched Brea's face turn ashy. "And it is known by the CVWA that you have been engaged with some dangerous people to stop the customer relationship improvement efforts. Is this true?"

Brea started to shake, thinking, '*I've gone too far this time. What have I done?*'

The others were watching her fear surface and took pity on her.

"Brea." Dani said, sitting down beside her. "Tell us what's going on. We want to help. It sounds like you're deep into a precarious situation. Is it true?"

"No. No, I don't know anything about crimes being committed. I'm not sure I even believe you." Brea shot back.

"I don't know all the details. Rob said I'm in danger too. If you know anything at all that could help, please don't hold back. Do you still work for Bellalto Rafting?" Anna replied impatiently.

"All I was doing was trying to keep the Marinetas from succeeding in their plans to share the water." Brea continued belligerently.

"You *live* in Marin, Brea," Glen responded tersely.

"When I'm Mayor, I'll be able to bring more prosperous enterprises to Marin. Besides, my long-term aspirations lie elsewhere. Marin is only a steppingstone."

"What makes you so sure that the people of Marin would want you as Mayor?" Glen asked.

"I'm working on something toward that end." She replied.

"Why do you want us to suffer more than we have?" Dani asked.

"That's not it. I-I have to leave now." Brea rose and headed toward her truck.

"It might not be safe for you to be alone. I'm inviting you and Anna to stay with me tonight." Dani called after her.

Brea stopped and turned back while opening her truck door. "Are you kidding me? I can defend myself." She sneered. Soon she was speeding down the drive to the highway, turning in the direction of Marin.

"Anna, you are welcome. Will you come?" Dani reiterated the invitation.

"I will. But first, I need to stop by my attorney's. I don't know what is happening in Bellalto beyond what Rob told me. Glen, if you care to join me, I'd appreciate it. It might involve the Council. We can call Rob back from his office."

"Good idea. Dani, would you mind stopping by my house to inform Meg why I'm going to be late?" Glen asked. "See you later Eric."

Chapter 45

Expose (the deeds of darkness). Ephesians 5:11

The young woman looked up. "We're here to see Tom Pettrie." Three men stood in front of her by Bellalto Rafting's receptionist desk with the Sheriff. She knew them all. Two were Marinetas and the other one was Tom's security detail. Protocol was to announce them to Mr. Pettrie and they were already moving in the direction of his office.

Just as she picked up the phone, the Sheriff turned around. "Don't call him please."

The Sheriff rapped twice on Tom's open door. "Hello Tom."

Tom turned from the window and watched as the men trooped in. "Gentlemen." His eyes leveled on his security agent.

"We've known each other for years and it pains me to come to you like this. I have evidence that you have been embezzling from the Water Authority for some time now."

Tom opened his mouth to deny the charges. He was interrupted as the Sherriff continued. "Furthermore, I have witnesses for that crime and for soliciting the commission of a violent crime against Rob Marineta." Turning to the agent, he said, "We're taking him into custody."

Silent as he was informed of his rights, Tom stared at Rob, who was not intimidated. As he was led out the door he turned around, "This is your fault. You should have left things alone. You'll never prove my guilt."

Sean arrived as Tom climbed into the unmarked police vehicle. With one look, he followed the car speaking into his phone. "Give me John."

"John, can you come to the police station fast? I'm following the Sheriff. They have Dad."

"Sean, I have no idea what's going on. I'm leaving now."

Found By the Water

Josh gave his statement and left when Tom was led to an interrogation room joined by his attorney. The litigation attorney for CVWA was also present with Rob. It would be a long evening for them. He texted his Dad that he'd see him in the morning. Then he left a message for Anna.

"This is Josh. I'm on my way to Marin. I'll stop by your house to give you an update. See you soon."

❧

Anna listened to the message as she exited her attorney's office with Glen. She left a counter message, "Meet me at Dani's."

Turning to Glen, "Josh is on his way. Would you come too?"

They pulled into Dani's at the same time Brea did. "I'm glad you changed your mind." Anna greeted her.

"I didn't change my mind. I came to give you my resignation letter."

The front door opened and Dani stepped out. "Let's do this inside. Please come in."

When they were seated, Brea handed Anna the paper. "This is my letter of resignation from the Council."

Anna read it quickly and passed it to Glen. "I think it's for the best. We accept your resignation. Here's a letter from my attorney asking for you to do that or face more serious consequences. We're still in the dark though, about your motives. Would you be willing to tell us what prompted you to practically libel yourself?"

"I told you! I think I can do a better job for this town as Council Chair. You're getting too soft."

"And I told you, it's because I learned that I wasn't alone in this world. I began seeking to know if God cared about me. I learned that he does; beyond anything I imagined. That understanding is changing me. I don't have to struggle through life on my own. He loves you too." Anna paused.

"I'm fine with who I am! I don't need God." Brea spat out. She looked to Glen for support.

"I depend on God's loving kindness and guidance, Brea. Meg does too. My faith in Christ has grown over the years. I live by his strength and truth." Glen explained. "I think there's more to your story. What is your connection to the Pettrie's, other than working for them?"

"I'm friends with Sean. But I know nothing of his father's criminal activities. He just wanted me around for information about what the

150

Found By the Water

Marinetas were doing. If you had remained in charge as usual, Anna, everything would have been fine."

"How can you say that when you know the town is in such bad shape?" Anna asked.

"It's not my town. I don't have a stake in Marin. There's nothing for me here. I've probably lost all my jobs by this time." Brea stated.

"Brea, can we pray with you before you leave?" Glen offered.

"No. I'm not interested. It's not for me." Brea stood. "I have a lot to do. Please leave me alone."

Over dinner after Josh and Meg arrived, he told them the details of Tom Pettrie's arrest. They prayed together for Tom, Sean, and Brea, and for good to come out of the unsettling situation. When Anna and Glen left, their next stop was the Farin' editorial office. The attorney had already sent a letter to the paper's owner.

Chapter 46

Because of His great love for us. Ephesians 2:4

Brea sped all the way to Bellalto after leaving Dani's. She called Sean a few times, frightened and mad. Driving directly to his house, she banged on the front door not caring how rude it was.

"What do you want Brea? This isn't a good time." Sean started to shut the door.

"Oh no you don't!" She shouted, preventing him from closing her out by shoving the door. "You owe me an explanation. I had no idea it was dangerous to help you."

"Why did you anyway Brea? You offered. I never asked you to do that. You haven't told me everything you were doing either. And unsuccessful, weren't you? Leave me alone. I mean it. I want nothing more to do with you!" The door slammed shut.

She stood there for a few minutes trying to control her anger and hold back tears, then drove to Bellalto Rafting headquarters. The building was locked up, dark, and the parking lot empty. Next, she headed back to Marin and parked at the Farin' building. Getting out of the truck, she saw Anna and Glen walk out the front door and quickly ducked back in, she bent low over the seat. *'There goes that job too.'*

Back home, self-incrimination turned to blaming others for her failure to succeed. *'I've been out-foxed. I need another-,'* her ringing phone cut off her thoughts.

"Hello Brea. Gracie here. Everything okay with you? I had the strongest sense to call you." Her sister greeted her.

"Gracie." Brea replied. "How do you do that? You always know when I'm in trouble."

"Ah, I was right again. What's going on this time?"

"It's a long story. Me being me, things backfiring. Seriously, how?"

Found By the Water

"Brea, you know it's the Holy Spirit looking out for you. He lets me know." Gracie gently chided. "Is it time to come home for a while? You can stay with me until you work it out."

Gracie was a woman of faith. The only sibling who believed in Jesus and the only one who cared about Brea in a helpful way. Repeatedly, she had been there for her, always hopeful that one day Brea would trust Jesus.

"Yes, Gracie. I'll come."

"I love you Brea. See you soon."

Chapter 47

You go before me and follow me. Psalm 139:5

Anna woke slowly the next morning at Dani's. Her sleep had been deeper and more restful than she had expected. She smiled with her eyes still closed as she remembered God loved her beyond measure.

A little while later as the coffee brewed. she looked at her phone. It was early but she needed to talk to her family.

"Morning Josh." she greeted him.

"Anna?" A sleepy voice answered.

"I have some good news to share with you and Rob. I forgot to mention it last night. Can you both meet me for lunch by the lake?" Anna invited. "My treat this time."

When they arrived at their table by the window, the two tired men greeted her like family. Over the meal, she told them about her prayer of faith in Jesus. "I understand so much more now than I did when we met that day, Josh. It's hard to believe it was only a few months ago. For the first time in my life, I know God loves me without reservation. I know the Holy Spirit will guide me now, according to the bible. I belong to his family too. How can I ever thank you for coming to Marin?"

Both men expressed their happiness for her new-found faith. Then the conversation turned to the arrest.

"It was a long night at the station." Rob said. "Tom continued to protest his guilt until, at the advice of his attorney, he stopped talking altogether."

"How did you learn about Brea?" Anna asked.

Found By the Water

"She's Sean's friend, not Tom's. I suspect she's been trying to be more than that. I don't think she knew anything about the threat on my life or the embezzlement." Rob replied. "She wanted to be useful and impress him."

"It also dove-tailed with her desire to oust me as Mayor and Council Chair. She is convinced she could do a better job. It explains a lot of ill will between us. She lost her chance. I doubt the community will trust her after learning of her activities. In the meantime, she's lost three jobs."

"She's a troubled woman, Anna. She needs to know Jesus." Josh said compassionately.

"We tried to help her but she didn't want it." Anna agreed.

"On another note, would you like to be there when we install Glen as a new CVWA Board member? We know that he and Eric have made enormous progress. It's a good time for Glen to join us for the next meeting."

"I would like that. Would you also invite his wife Meg?" Anna asked. "Glen and I think that Dani would be a good fit as Brea's replacement. We're going to talk to the rest of the Council and see what they think."

"Have you mentioned yet my invitation to visit the ruins of the first Bellalto settlement?" Josh asked.

"Who's had time?" She said with a grin. "I'll do it."

Chapter 48

I have named you, though you have not known me. Isaiah 45:4

A nna was back at her secret refuge by the river. She thought, *'Elianna died believing God would answer her prayers for reconciliation. I am living proof he did.'* She pulled two leather-bound books from the car and sat in her hammock chair. One was her bible and the other was a journal. Without Elianna's journal they would not have known God's faithfulness to answer ancient prayers in precisely the way he had. It was time for Anna to record her own story.

"Lord, I hope it will help those who come after me to seek you, through Jesus Christ, and believe." Anna turned to the first pristine page and wrote:

> "My name is Elianna Marin. At my birth I received a name that intertwines with a woman of great faith, Elianna Marineta. I knew that Elianna was a family name and it was an honor to receive it. I understand far more now because I have met my namesake through her own journal. Our name means "God has answered me." Elianna Marineta had a strong desire for her family's reconciliation through forgiveness of each other and acceptance of Jesus.
>
> I, Elianna Marin, have received the answer to her prayer a century and a half later. Her journal is a testament that she died in faith believing that God is faithful although she did not see the answer in her lifetime.
>
> The bible says that God's faithfulness continues through all generations and that one generation commends God's works to another.[21]
>
> I can see that my life is a testament to both these verses. I asked God one small question, without knowing it was a prayer. "God, do you see me?" My deepest needs, although I did not know it, were to know God and belong in a loving family. When I was alone, he gave me friends and family who knew him. I asked for water and he gave me a river of Grace.
>
> He found me by the water.

THE END

APPENDIX

Bible References

*Version or lack of: Refer to Copyright Page

Footnote	Page	Scripture	*Version
1	xi	John 4:1-26	
2	45	Proverbs 15:1	NKJV
3	56	Isaiah 55:8	NKJV
4	58	Romans 8:27	
5	66	1 Samuel 16:7	
6	67	Proverbs 23:7	NKJV
7	75	James 1:3	
8	112	Jeremiah 31:3	
9	132	Genesis 16:13	
10	135	Psalm 139.13	
11	135	Genesis 17:19, 28:14, 49:10	
12	135	2 Samuel 7:12-13	
13	135	Isaiah 7:14, Micah 5:2	
14	135	Isaiah 35:5-6	
15	135	Isaiah 53	
16	136	Matthew 1:18-25	
17	136	John 5:19	
18	136	2 Timothy 3:16	
19	136	Ephesians 2:8-9	
20	136	Romans 3:23	
21	157	Psalm 119:90,145:4	

Acknowledgements

For our Reader Team's valuable insights.
Denise Bernson, Colleen Hall, Jocelyn Kurtz, Uta Milewski, Lisa
Varco, and Alice Weisbecker

*For the beautiful art adorning these pages, the cover design and
creation.*
Gary Spears and Uta Milewski

For editing to exacting standards.
Jocelyn Kurtz and Lisa Varco

For the firefighting experience and knowledge.
Christopher McAviney

*For all the encouragement and prayers from countless friends. We are
grateful for all who helped us create this book. Thank You.*

Until We Meet Again

Our prayer is for you to know God's love in all your circumstances.

To discern His heart in the matters of today.

To follow the Holy Spirit's direction, as you seek guidance and revelation.

May He meet you on the road that leads away from your true purpose and walk with you to the destination of His choosing.

For those He has called to join with you on the way; may all of you heed His call and keep divine appointments.

For your hearts to be full of His grace and your voices declare gratitude for the plans He has for your future.

Thank you for reading Found By the Water.
Shirley A Genovese and Cynthia Gibbs

The Authors

S hirley A Genovese learned at a young age the power of stories to transport her to different times and places while snuggled up to her Mom and Grandma as they read to her. She still remembers her joy when learning to read and her spirit grew wings. Through books she could go anywhere at any time. Her love of stories has endured throughout her life. She hopes to impart that same joy to others.

Shirley earned her bachelor's degree in Business Management and Accounting at New York State University. She inspires the best from those she engages with and has learned much about human nature and the struggles people face. She writes to entertain and encourage. Shirley presents truths in a way that can shift perspectives, stimulate spiritual growth, and introduce new adventures.

Shirley uses stories to illuminate spiritual life when writing for her WordPress blog "Eyes to See Ears to Hear". She authored a devotional book entitled *A Confident Expectation 40 Hope-Full Conversations*, published in 2019, highlighting the hope to be found in Jesus Christ.

Website: shirleyagenovese.com

C ynthia Gibbs was passionate about two things growing up: her desire to be a registered nurse, and her love of the written word. After realizing her calling to be a nurse, she has been practicing the profession for over four decades with dedication and pride. Along the way, Cynthia met and married her soulmate, and together they raised two sons, who provided them with two lovely "daughters in love" and four wonderful grandchildren. Cynthia and her husband now live in the Upstate of South Carolina, enjoying a milder climate from her native New York State.

Always an avid reader, Cynthia had a secret longing to be a writer. Family and career delayed that wish and provided a wealth of experience from which to draw. Her wish is that through her stories, others will recognize that the joys and struggles of life are something we all have in common, and that God is always the answer.

CPSIA information can be obtained
at www.ICGtesting.com
Printed in the USA
BVHW081221040521
606414BV00004B/444